# A

# Truth

## SLICE Book 1

Cherron Riser

Cherronriser@gmail.com

Printed in the United States of America

First Printing, February 26, 2016

www.facebook.com/cherronriser

Editing by Kelly Hartigan (XterraWeb)

Cover Design by Paradox Book Cover Designs

ISBN- 978-1530175444

*Cherron Riser*
www.cherronriser.com

# Acknowledgements

This is for my Mother, my Aunt Debbie, my Uncle Joe, my Grandmother, and all of the others who have supported my work from the start. I love all of you so much! Thank you for believing in me.

# A SLICE of Truth

SLICE Book 1

# Table of Contents

# Before the Chase

# Chapter One

Shifting from their bird forms to that of men, they sat down on the ground behind the dumpster, panting after having run so much. It had been days since they last slept, and energy was running on an all-time low. Three days ago, the twins, Jax and Jericho, had watched as their parents were dragged away by men with guns and Tasers. Never had either of them been more frightened. Their parents had sacrificed their lives to save them. Now they belonged to SLICE, Supernatural Laboratories for the Investigation of Chaotic Entities, a government agency designed for the sole purpose of hunting and capturing shifters for their own sick pleasure.

Since their parent's capture, the brothers had run nonstop, often shifting into the form of birds to fly and escape more quickly. They wanted to get as far away from home as possible. When they had been children, their parents had told them of the people who hunted their kind, but neither of them believed it would really happen. They had lived too far from town and kept to themselves. Why would anyone care about what they did? Oh, how foolish they had been.

"What are we going to do, brother? We can't keep running like this," Jax asked, his breath coming hard and deep, making his already gravelly voice sound harsher. They both knew it was long past time to get real rest or risk being too weak to fight off anyone who came for them.

"We have to. Those guys weren't kidding around. I'm not going to risk them catching us, not now," Jericho answered, leaning his head back against the brick wall. He knew it was fear driving him, but he couldn't help himself. "We are going to need to find a way to make money though. We will need to sleep, shower, and eat eventually. Like you said, we can't keep running like this."

"Yeah, I'm starving, and I am tired of dumpster diving," Jax responded, looking over at his brother.

Jericho heard Jax's stomach growl and groaned. Wasted food out of fast food dumpsters was no way to live, but that had been the only food they had been able to find in the cities. They were often chased off by irate store managers or policemen who thought they were trying to break the law. All they were trying to do, however, was keep up a bit of strength. As shifters, they had the ability to transform into animals. However, this required a large amount of energy that demanded to be fed on a regular basis.

In their human or natural form, they both had inky black hair, crystal blue eyes, and pale skin. However, that was where the similarities ended. Jax was a huge mass of a man, even at eighteen. He was tall and broad and wore his hair long. His face was covered in a thick scratchy beard that blocked his youthful appearance. Despite his human form, Jax held the heart of an animal and even had the power to shift into a true beast like nothing seen in nature. Jax was more animal than man.

Jericho, on the other hand, was lean and wiry. He kept his hair short and his face clean, though being on the road had given him a scruffy look. His forms were more common like wolves or birds, nothing as extravagant as Jax. When it came down to it, Jericho had cunning, unlike his brother's brute nature.

Because of Jax's animal nature, Jericho was sure he would have to take care of his brother. Neither of them had spent a lot of time within cities; however, Jericho could at least hold a conversation without making the person he was talking to piss themselves. Deciding they had no other choice, Jericho took a deep breath and patted his brother on the leg. Looking at their surroundings, Jericho stood and headed for the end of the street. "Stay here and lay low. Don't do anything or talk to anyone. I will be back as soon as I can."

He wasn't sure what he was going to do to get money and find food, but he would figure it out. Moving toward the street, he looked left and then right. People were walking everywhere, oblivious to the world around them. They carelessly wandered about, unaware of the dangers so close to them lurking in plain sight. Most would never know the fear and pain Jericho and his brother had just faced. It almost made him sick that they would never feel what he had felt all because they were human. It was a luxury Jericho would never get, and it infuriated him.

Pride surged in Jericho for a moment as he pushed his wrathful thoughts away and began to think of ways to get money. They had not been raised to be beggars. Everything they had they worked for. Now he was faced with the choice to either beg or watch as he and his brother starved. Finding some resolve, Jericho approached an older man wearing a long wool coat. To Jericho, the man appeared to be some sort of businessman, which meant he might have some money. With a racing heart, he tapped the older gentleman on the shoulder and waited to see if he would turn around.

"Can I help you?" the man asked, looking Jericho up and down with eyes that made him feel uncomfortable. Jericho took a step back as he tried to formulate the right words to say. No one had ever prepared him for a life like this, and the agony of stooping so low had caused his mouth to go dry and his heart to race.

"Umm, yes, sir, my brother and I just lost our parents, and we are starving. I was wondering if I could borrow some money or even do some work for you and earn the money," Jericho finally said, licking his lips and rubbing the back of his neck. The constant shaking of his nerves made it hard for him to focus, and he took another deep breath to relieve some of the tension.

The man took his time contemplating his request. Now that Jericho had a better look at him, he saw he had to have been in his mid-fifties. His hair was mostly gray with a few specks of the brown from his youth. Crow's feet graced the corners of the gentleman's eyes, and deeper lines had taken residence on his brow. He was still a handsome man, having aged well, but was aged all the same. However, it was the way his eerie dark eyes kept evaluating him that made Jericho question his decision to speak to him.

"You know, I think I can help you out. I have something I need taken care of. Do you mind coming with me to my office for a few minutes? It shouldn't take too long, and then you can be on your way. I will pay you fifty dollars," the man explained, a friendly smile broadening over his face.

Jericho knew it was a risky move to go, but he had to take the chance. Looking back at the alleyway where he had left his brother, he then turned back to the man and nodded his acceptance. "Yeah, I can do that. Lead the way."

With a crook on the edge of his smile, the man led them toward one of the tall buildings nearby. Atlanta was a much larger city than anything Jericho had ever seen before. It was intimidating to someone who had lived in the country for most of his life, but larger cities were easier to get lost in. It was one of the main reasons they had chosen to head for the city and continued to do so in their travels.

Reaching the building, the two of them slipped into a back door and began to ascend the stairs. Sweat formed on Jericho's palms, and the pounding of his heart echoed in his ears. Something was wrong. Every one of his instincts was telling him to run, but all he could think about was his brother. There was no way he would let his brother starve another day. With fifty dollars, they could eat and find a place to sleep for a night. He would have to ignore his irrational fears and press on.

The office the man led him to was at the end of a hall. There was not much inside, a desk, a couple of chairs, and some bookshelves. On the desk were a few family photos and random pieces of office supplies. Jericho's breath came more quickly as the door clicked shut, and the man walked around to face him once more. The entire way, nothing had been said about what Jericho would be doing for him, which only added to Jericho's unease.

"So, what is it you would like me to do for you, Mr. ...?" Jericho asked, shoving his hands in his jeans pockets and looking around to keep from letting his nervousness get the best of him.

"Let's not bother with names. It is better that way," the man explained, shrugging off his coat and laying it over the back of his leather office chair. Slowly he walked back toward Jericho, unbuttoning the ends of his sleeves. Reaching past Jericho, the man locked the door so no one could walk into the office, and once again, Jericho's heart rate accelerated. His mouth became parched, and dizziness consumed him. What the hell had he just gotten himself into?

With the door locked, the man stood before him and smiled at him. He reached to his back pocket and pulled out a few bills. Holding them out to Jericho, the man let his eyes roam over Jericho's body. Jericho took a step back and found himself pressed against the cold wooden door, but his hand involuntarily took the money. They needed it so badly, but he had a feeling he would be selling his soul for it.

"Okay, we don't have to exchange names. That is fine by me. Now, umm, what is it you wanted me to do? I don't want to keep you from your work too long," Jericho asked, licking his lips and swallowing hard. His throat was closing up and his body was shaking.

"Don't be so nervous, my boy. I'm not going to hurt you," the man answered moving in closer. He reached up and stroked Jericho's cheek before leaning in and breathing deeply. It was as if the man was trying to memorize his scent the same way an animal would. "I just want you to take off your clothes for a bit, and I'm going to make you feel good. It shouldn't take too long then you can be on your way."

What kind of shitty luck did Jericho have in life? If losing his parents weren't enough, now this man was propositioning him for something. Jericho had been raised away from people. He had never been naked in front of someone else before, and though he knew about sex and such things, he had never experienced them. "I ... I have never done anything like that before."

"It is all right. You don't have to do anything but stand there and look like you're pretty self. I will take care of the rest." The man reached and began to touch Jericho's body. He pulled at his clothes and worked to strip him, and Jericho let him. He had no idea what to do or how to act. It was as if it was happening to someone else and not him.

Jericho instead looked at the ceiling and tried to keep his breath steady as the man did all he wanted with his body. The whole time, he kept his mind focused on the fact he was doing this for his brother. A few minutes of his time and they would have food and shelter for a little while. It would be worth it, and it wouldn't take much. Just a small part of his soul, and he and his brother could eat and sleep.

***

He didn't like this. Jax was not the type of man to be babied, and that was exactly how his brother made him feel. There was little he could do about it in the moment, though. Jericho was gone, and if Jax left from where he was at, they could be separated. After seeing his parents dragged away like criminals, the last thing he wanted was to lose his brother. Bending his legs up, Jax rested his arms on his knees and let his head fall back against the wall. Another loud growl sounded from his stomach, and he twisted his nose up at the sound. Never had he known hunger like this before.

Nor had he experienced such fear. Every sound he heard and shadow he saw made him think someone was after him. Their home, the place they had lived since he was a child, had been trashed. Parts of it had even been burned as he and his brother worked to escape. Even now, Jax could smell the smoke and hear the sounds of his mother screaming. It was a haunting nightmare that would plague him the rest of his life.

"They sacrificed themselves for us," he whispered, feeling a mix of anger and pain. Pain didn't come easy to the large man, and he wanted to fight against it, so anger became his best friend. It was so much easier to just be angry than to feel all of these other foreign emotions he had never been made to feel before.

Jericho told him all the time that he was more an animal. He had a feeling that being an animal was not going to help him here. The city was huge and full of people. Yeah, he and people had never spoken the same language, and he was sure that was a large part of the reason Jericho had decided to treat him the way he was. It didn't make it right though. Nor did it mean he wanted Jericho to do all the talking for him. Jericho was not his father, no matter how much he felt like he was in charge. Being two minutes older didn't count for much.

Jax shifted on the hard ground, trying to keep his butt from falling asleep. Earlier he had seen Jericho walk down the street with an older man. The hair on the back of his neck had stood up at the sight of his brother with that man. Something was off, but he had no idea what it was. He knew Jericho could take care of himself, so he let it go, but part of him wondered if maybe he should have done something. Now his brother was God only knew where. In a city this size, Jax would have a Hell of a time trying to find him.

Maybe after a good meal, Jax could look for some sort of work to help out. Sure, they were only passing through, but if they both did something for money, then they would have an easier time of it. Jax was strong. He was sure there were labor jobs he could get his hands on. Either way, he had to do something. There was no way

in Hell he would let his brother do everything.
Enough people had sacrificed for him already.

# Chapter Two

Jericho was still shaking by the time he got back to the ally he had left his brother at. Slowly he made his way down the darkened walkway before peeking around the dumpster. Jax was still sitting there, his eyes closed as if he were trying to get some rest, but the moment Jericho walked up, Jax's nose wrinkled. With Jax so close to his animal side, he had always had keener senses, and embarrassment rushed through Jericho thinking of what Jax might pick up on him.

"You smell strange. You smell like a human has been—" Jax began to say as he looked up at him.

"I have money. Let's go get some food," Jericho interrupted, not wanting to talk about what had happened. As it was, Jericho wanted to scrub himself down with steel wool and boiling water. His skin was crawling, but he would never regret it. They would eat tonight, and that was more important than his dignity.

Jax didn't say a word, got up, and dusted himself off. Stretching for a moment, he then moved closer, and they walked out of the alley. Jericho knew his brother could read him. They had always been able to read each other. So if Jericho didn't want to talk about something, Jax was not going to pester him about it. Instead he walked next to him in companionable silence.

They wandered up and down streets for quite some time until finally reaching some hole-in-the-wall diner. Opening the door, they stepped into a dark, greasy restaurant with black and white checkered floors. There was a bar expanding across most of the room with booths lining the walls. It was dingy and gross, which meant it would be cheap. Finding a seat in the corner, the two of them pulled out menus so they could decide what they wanted to eat.

"I have fifty, so we have enough to eat and find some cheap roach motel for the night. I think I saw somewhere not far from here that we could stay at. I want a shower so bad," Jericho said as he perused the menu. It had all the usual diner favorites, burgers, meatloaf, chicken fingers, and breakfast food. It was nothing special, but after several days of dumpster food, it all looked like five-star cuisine.

"You don't have to take care of everything, Jericho. I'm not a baby. I can help you with this," Jax whispered, glancing at him from over the menu.

The waitress, a plump middle-aged woman who smelled of smoke and looked less than amused to be at work, came and took their orders. With little enthusiasm, the woman scribbled down their orders of burgers and fries and went to collect their sodas.

"I know, but things are different in the city. You are used to the country, and when we are in the country, you are going to help a lot. But you have to admit that you will scare off people in the city. They are not used to people like us as it is, but you are an animal, and they will pick up on that," Jericho answered.

Emotions flared in Jax's eyes, and Jericho could feel the energy surging off him. His brother was a proud man, just like Jericho was. He didn't want to hear his brother say he wasn't useful. "I can do more than you are giving me credit for. I can do labor jobs or something like that. I will not have you taking care of me like some sort of child. We are brothers, and we will face this as brothers."

Jericho decided it wasn't worth arguing about, so he nodded in agreement. They had been through a lot over the last few days, and he just wanted to relax and not think about it all. After a good meal and some sleep, he was sure his brother would calm down and the two of them could move forward trying to find a place they would be safe.

\*\*\*

The scent on his brother was extremely thick, and the way he was shaking only made Jax angrier. Jericho didn't want to talk about what had happened, but he was sure it was bad. He had never seen his brother acting in such a way. Now they were settled in the hotel room, and Jax had watched his brother rush to the shower. There was a glimpse of some red marks on his brother's skin, and it broke Jax's heart. He should have been there for him. He should not have let his brother go.

It had not been too long since he and Jericho had started talking about carnal urges and the desire to meet women. They were young, and their bodies were waking up to such desires, but neither of them had the opportunity to act on them. No, it had all been left up to fantasies in their minds and cold dips in the river.

They weren't boys anymore, though, and he had a feeling his brother was more a man now than he had been when they woke up that morning. Jericho looked and felt different in ways that bothered Jax. Moving about the room, he sat on the edge of the bed and began to strip off his clothes. He would let Jericho have all the time he needed before taking his turn with the shower. Honestly, with how tired he was, he might wait until the morning before cleaning up.

Once he was in nothing more than his boxers, he pulled back the covers of one of the beds and lay down. It was nice to be in a bed after running for so long. His brother might call him an animal, and most days he was, but that didn't mean he couldn't appreciate a nice comfortable bed and the comforts a human life came with.

"You're not getting a shower?" Jericho asked as he walked out of the bathroom. He had dressed again, covering up his body as he dried his hair, just one more thing different about his brother. Neither of them ever slept in much unless it was necessary.

"I'm going to wait until the morning. I am too tired to mess with it right now. All I want is some good sleep. Maybe tomorrow I can find some work," Jax answered watching as Jericho got into the bed fully dressed. "You going to tell me about what happened today?"

Jericho stiffened in the other bed and then let out a deep breath. "I just went and did some busy work for this office guy. It really wasn't a big deal, and he paid me. It was better than begging people to give me a dollar until I had enough for us to buy a dollar menu cheeseburger."

It was a lie. Jax could tell when his brother was lying, just like he was sure Jericho could do with him. It came with being more than just brothers. It came with being twins. There were no secrets between them, and the fact Jericho was trying to keep one from him now bothered him more than Jericho trying to baby him. He wanted his brother to be honest and open with him so he could help him.

"You know you can talk to me. I won't judge or criticize. I just want to know. I want to help," Jax growled, trying not to let his anger flare into his words.

"There is nothing to tell. I went with the dude, helped him do some stuff, and left him happy. What more do you want from me. Look, it's late, you want to shower in the morning, and personally I am exhausted. How about we get some sleep, and we can figure out the rest tomorrow.

Another brush off, and his brother rolled away from him. The distance was immeasurable. Sure, Jericho was in the room, but it wasn't the same. Now it felt like he had not only lost his parents, but his brother as well. There was no point in arguing. Jericho was not going to talk about what had happened, and he had made a good point. Staying up all night arguing over it would only cost them sleep in an actual bed. Jax rolled away as well and curled into his pillow. A good night's sleep was just what the both of them needed. Maybe his brother would talk to him after that.

# Chapter Three

They had spent a couple of days in Atlanta, but they were too afraid to stay anywhere for very long, so they moved on. For months they traveled from city to city, never staying in one place more than a couple of days. Now they were in a small town on the coast outside of Myrtle Beach, South Carolina. The ocean breeze left Jericho's lips tasting salty, but the warm wind was nice. He would not complain about being in paradise.

As they came into the town, they passed a constructions site. Without saying a word to him, Jax walked away from Jericho for a moment to speak with the other men. Jericho felt his heart race as he watched his brother speak to the foreman. For as long as he could remember, Jericho had always taken the lead when it came to dealing with humans. To see Jax stepping up and trying to find a way to take care of them worried him. What if Jax scared the Hell out of the humans? Word would spread quickly, and SLICE would be on their tails again.

After a few moments, Jax walked back with a smug smile on his face. "So, the foreman said they needed someone to work for them. I am to report at five in the morning. They pay by the day."

"Well, that will be good." Jericho let out the breath he had been holding as the two of them went about walking farther through town. Jericho shoved his hands in his pants pockets and closed his eyes for a moment, using his other senses to keep himself from falling or getting hurt.

"Yeah, I told you that I could help out and get us money. You have to let me be a man, too. Everything doesn't have to fall on your shoulders," Jax answered, his voice more a growl as he tried to talk softly.

Jericho was relieved more than he wanted to admit. Ever since that first day in Atlanta, Jericho had felt himself slipping. He had spent nights out on the streets making money off of lecherous old men while Jax stayed behind, ignorant to what Jericho had been up to. Even as they traveled, Jericho would try to find work to ensure they had money to keep them fed and clean. Jax never asked what Jericho did for the money, but he was sure his brother suspected. However, Jericho didn't have it in him to really talk about it.

Passing by a small beachside restaurant, Jericho heard his stomach start to growl and looked toward his brother. Pulling out what remained of his cash, Jericho counted it out to see if they had enough to eat in a sit-down place or if they would need to hit up the dollar menu again. Thirty four dollars, it might very well be enough.

"What do you think about us getting some real food for a change? If you are going to get paid tomorrow, then we can make do tonight. The beach looks nice, and we can always sleep under the pier or something," Jericho asked as he smiled at his brother.

"I could use a good meal. I don't think my stomach likes this diet of fast food we have been torturing ourselves with. If I am going to do well working, I think it would be best if I eat something with more to it than fat and grease." Jax reached out and opened the door for the two of them.

Inside, waitresses were rushing around filling orders and talking to customers. The room was warm and welcoming, painted beige with accents of blue, giving the feel of being by the ocean. A bank of windows lined the back wall, which opened up to a beachside deck for extra seats. The aroma of the food being cooked made Jericho even hungrier than he had been before, and he put his hand on his stomach to curb the hunger pains.

"Hello, welcome to The Tide Diner, I'm Mallory, follow me, please," a waitress said, catching Jericho off guard. He looked to the voice and found a young woman with sunshine for hair and sky blue eyes. There was a dusting of freckles on her face, and her lips were the perfect shade of pink. Looking over at his brother, he tried hard to hide his attraction to the girl. They did not have time to get messed up with things like this.

Walking after Mallory, he took a seat in the booth she took them to. His eyes never left her, though, as he watched her place the menus and silverware down for them. "Our special today is the shrimp and grits, this is our lunch menu, but we serve breakfast all day. What can I get you to drink?"

Jax wasted no time asking for a soda, but Jericho took his time for a moment. He looked up and ginned at Mallory. She was giving him the most beautiful smile he had ever seen, and it made his heart flutter a bit. "I think I will just do some tea. Thank you."

Jax was arching a brow at him when Jericho turned back to his brother. Or at least, Jericho thought that was the look he was being given. It was sometimes hard to tell with all the hair on his brother's face. "What the Hell was all that about?" Jax asked bluntly.

"What? She's pretty. I know life is hard, but that doesn't make me blind. You and me have been living in the country all of our lives, then we go and run away from home. I feel like we never have any fun. Don't you want to experience life a little?" Jericho answered, an amused look stretching over his handsome face.

Mallory came back a moment later with the drinks, and Jax began to mumble out his order of country fried steak with greens and cornbread. Jericho hadn't looked at the menu yet. Not wanting to appear like a dork, he ordered the daily special. Once she was gone, he looked back at Jax, his face frozen in a mix of mischievous excitement.

"Look, she is pretty, and I get that whole carnal urge thing, but we really don't have time for this. We will only be able to stay for a few days, and then we are going to be gone. What happens if you start messing around with that girl and get attached to her?" Jax offered up in a somber, aggravated tone.

"I won't get attached. I just want a little bit of time to feel normal. It isn't right that we always have to hide and pretend. Sometimes I wish I would have been born human. Then I wouldn't have to deal with all of this crap," Jericho answered, leaning in more so no one else could hear their conversation. The energy inside of him surged in defiance to his words. Truthfully he would miss the power he held if it left him, but it didn't change his desire to be able to live without fear of being pulled away from everyone and everything he loved.

"Okay, what happens if you let yourself get a little frisky with the girl, and we leave, and she gets pregnant? You won't ever know, because we will be gone, and she won't know about us being shifters. Her baby would more than likely be a shifter too, and then what. You going to be able to live with yourself if you ever find out that your bastard child was taken from its mother, or worse, they were both killed. Sorry, I don't think that is something I could live with right now. Urges or not, I will deal with keeping us alive, and fuck the rest. My left hand and I have become good friends when it comes to dealing with those urges." Jax finished off his soda as he gave his lecture, one Jericho really didn't want to hear, regardless of the fact his brother had a very good point.

Jax couldn't possibly understand what was happening to him. All of these late night dalliances, doing things he didn't really want to do but needed to for money, had awakened his body in ways he hadn't understood before. Sure, like most boys, he had rubbed one out in the shower or late at night in bed, but it wasn't the same. Now the craving to be with someone, someone who wanted him for more than just a cheap thrill, was strong. He wanted to know how much better it would be if it were with someone who liked him or even cared about him. The idea of having a mutual attraction and desire was a hunger Jericho craved more than anything. It wasn't like he was looking for forever, just a few moments of normalcy.

However, his brother had made a good point. If he got Mallory pregnant all because he just wanted to have a good time, he would never be able to live with himself. It would put them all in danger, and, more than likely, get Mallory killed. Jericho was many things, but he would never hurt a woman like that. It didn't mean the selfish side of him didn't want to find a way to make this work. His face falling with his turbulent thoughts, he sat back, but his eyes kept going to watch the girl. There seemed to be a halo of light surrounding her, and it drew him in more and more.

When she came with their food, Jericho couldn't hold back anymore. "So, my brother and I are new here in town. Any advice on what we could do to pass the time? He starts a job tomorrow, but we have all night tonight."

He watched as pink chased over Mallory's cheeks, and the heat she put off nearly seared his skin. For a moment she played with the corner of her apron and thought about his question. "Well, it is Friday night, so a lot of us are going out to the pier to hang out. If you guys want, you could come and hang out with us. It isn't anything special, just a bunch of us drinking and being silly, but it is fun."

Jax gave Jericho a stern look, but Jericho ignored it. No matter how true Jax's words were, Jericho could not shake his selfish need to just be a teenager and enjoy some time with a pretty girl. "Sure, that would be awesome. Thanks, Mallory. What time do you get off from here? We can just meet you here if you would like. Well, unless your boyfriend is coming to get you."

Her sweet giggle sent a pulse of electricity down his spine, and Jax rolled his eyes before starting to shovel food into his mouth. "I don't have a boyfriend. I get off at nine. I will look forward to it." She turned and walked off.

Pride burned through Jericho, and he smiled even wider as he began to eat his meal. He couldn't even taste it; his thoughts were simply far too distracted. Before they left, Mallory brought them both a piece of apple pie à la mode and gave Jericho a wink before leaving the ticket at the table. Jericho snatched up the small paper and saw she had not charged them for the pie or drinks and had given them half-price dinners. With that discount, he would have a little money to get good and cleaned up before the night.

# Chapter Four

Jax and Jericho had found a truck stop that had shower facilities inside and managed to procure some time to wash up and shave. It wasn't the best way to go about getting ready for a date, but it worked well enough. Jax was still not amused with their plans, but he had decided to tag along and make sure Jericho didn't do something stupid.

Now that they were clean, the two of them headed for the diner again. Jericho could feel the tension in his brother, and for good reasons, but he couldn't shake the feeling he had inside of him. He had to do this. He had to find a way to erase all the nameless faces that haunted his dreams ever since that first man in Atlanta took him to his office. Jax didn't know, nor would he understand if Jericho were to tell him. For as much of an animal as he could be, Jax held within him a big heart and noble sensibility. He would insist they could find another way to get money and take care of themselves, but Jericho wasn't so sure and knew he could earn money with his body.

42

Reaching the Tide Diner, Jericho smiled as he saw Mallory stepping out from behind the building. She had changed from her work uniform and now wore a short black skirt and red tank top. Her eyes were darker now from the makeup she had applied, and her lips were a deep red. If she had been pretty before, she was gorgeous now. Jax grumbled something next to him, but Jericho was too entranced by the woman before him to be bothered with his brother's negative attitude.

"Hey, you made it! I wasn't sure you would really show," Mallory exclaimed, coming over and giving Jericho a huge hug. He couldn't help but breathe in her sweet scent, which reminded him of suntan oil and ocean salt, and bask in the warm, soft feel of her body. Yeah, he was young and horny; there wasn't much he could do about that.

When Mallory pulled away, she tried to hug Jax, but he made a growling noise, and she thought better of it. Shaking his head at his brother, Jericho took Mallory's hand so they could head for the pier. "Yeah, we got settled a bit and then freshened up before coming back. I was glad you invited us. We don't really know anyone here."

Mallory's smile widened and Jericho was sure his mouth started to water. He let his thumb run over her silky skin as she led them toward where her friends would be. "That is good. It is always nice to be settled and comfortable. So, do you guys live with your parents? What brought you to South Carolina?"

Jericho knew she was just making small talk, but the pain that stabbed through his heart was powerful. He was sure Jax felt it as well. Looking at his brother, he saw that same pain deep in the large man's animal eyes. It was almost an angry pain, and Jericho could relate. They had been running so much that neither of them had really been able to mourn the loss of their parents. "We just lost our parents, so we are sort of traveling to clear our heads," Jericho answered, his voice taking on a solemn tone.

Next to him, Mallory gasped and covered her mouth. Her steps stopped and she turned to him with genuine concern and empathy on her face. "I am so sorry. I didn't know." She took a moment to hug him again and even reached out and rubbed Jax's arm. To Jericho's surprise, Jax didn't pull away from the obviously unwelcome contact. Instead he stood there and let the girl comfort him in her own small way. It made Jericho wonder if maybe his brother understood humans better than Jericho gave him credit for. But then Jax growled and moved away, and Jericho shook his head. So much for that thought.

"It's all right. Come on. I don't want to think about that right now," Jericho said, taking her hand and pulling her along. He could see the lights from where the party was at, so he made his way toward it, not wanting to explain about his parents. It wasn't all right. It would never be all right, but he couldn't tell her the truth about it without explaining things she would not understand. Mallory was a human thinking with human knowledge. Nothing in her life would help her comprehend what Jax and Jericho had gone through.

Music started to fill the air, combined with the sound of people laughing and chatting. Jericho could see Jax's nostrils flare from next to him and knew he would rather not spend his time with a bunch of drunken teenagers on the beach. Next to him, Jericho felt Mallory start to bounce as a cheer of excitement left her, and she raced to hug another girl. This girl had darker skin and hair, which made her look exotic. The girls bounced as they hugged, and then Mallory pulled the girl toward them.

"Desiree, this is Jericho and his brother Jax. They just got to town, and I thought it would be nice for them to meet some people and have fun," Mallory explained to the girl. Those dark eyes looked from one to the other of them, and then a soft smile formed on her lips. There was a hint of daring mischievousness in the girl's eyes that made Jericho wonder what kind of things Desiree liked to get into.

"It is nice to meet you. Come on, we have some beer and sodas. My dad is the foreman working on that building over there. I am always able to get someone to buy me beer," Desiree said and turned to walk back to the party. Her black dress was too short, and Jericho could easily tell she wasn't wearing anything under it. Turning to Jax, he saw a mix of lust and worry in his brother's eyes, and it made him chuckle thinking his brother might quickly begin to understand Jericho's position on things.

"I don't need to make a fool of myself in front of the foreman's daughter," Jax grumbled under his breath. He turned his head away so his watching the girl wasn't obvious and shoved his hands deep into his pockets.

"Then don't. Play it cool and make sure none of these other jerks treat her bad. Be her big, bad savior and all that. I'm going to go dance and get a beer. Come on, the night is young and so are we," Jericho answered with a bit of laughter in his voice and then raced to catch up with Mallory.

When he reached the group, Jericho was handed a beer, and he instantly put on his most devilish grin. Already a couple of the girls were watching him, but he kept his attention on Mallory. Desiree seemed to enjoy the attention she got from several of the boys there, so Jericho didn't mind taking her friend's attention away from her. Jax sat away from the group, drinking beer and staring into the fire. Jericho could feel the restlessness in his brother, but the selfish side of him kept him perusing his night of debauchery and fun with the group and not paying any attention to Jax.

After a couple of drinks, Mallory pulled Jericho into her so they could dance. Over the last couple of months, Jericho had learned a lot about how his body moved, and he put those skills to use. The animal inside of him helped as well, giving him better grace and agility in his movements. His hands slid over her luscious curves, and he breathed in her tropical scent. It was an incredible relief to be close to this girl. Jericho wasn't sure if it was Mallory in particular or the fact that he wanted something that felt real. Either way, he was lost to it and to her.

As he turned Mallory in his arms, his hands slid up her back, and his fingers sank deep into her hair. For several heartbeats, their eyes locked in a heated stare, and he swore he stopped breathing. Then she moved into him, and he was compelled to do the same as their bodies pressed tightly against each other. Electricity sparked through his veins with the first brush of her lips against his. The kiss quickly grew, and he moaned into her mouth. All he could think about was how, out of all of his encounters, he had never enjoyed a kiss like that before. She tasted like honey, and the sweetness of it made him more intoxicated than any amount of beer ever would.

His head clouded up, and he began to move her farther under the pier. Several of the teens had split off into couples and found hidden places along the beach and pier to hide and make out. This was a first for Jericho, and he blocked out everyone around them as he experienced the first taste of this beautiful girl. He had never experienced such a tantalizing kiss in all of his life, and heat built up higher and higher in his body, bringing forth a primal instinct in him. He slammed Mallory against one of the pillars, lifting her so her legs would wrap around him and his body would press even more tightly against hers.

"You are such an incredible kisser. I could kiss you like this all night," Mallory breathed, arching back as his lips sent a scorching trail down her neck. Jericho could not get enough of the taste of her and the warmth of her skin. The sound of her voice thick with desire made his body tighten more, and he longed to push this to a place much further.

"I've never kissed anyone before," Jericho answered, nibbling on the soft flesh at the curve of her neck. Her body shivered in his arms as he worked her sensitive skin, and it made a sense of pride burst through every cell of his body and soul.

Mallory pulled away and looked at him. Her eyes seemed to pierce him, and he was suddenly nervous about what he was doing. "I would have never known. You are so handsome and sexy. You feel like—"

Jericho didn't want to come off like a virgin. He wasn't one. His virginity was only intact when it came to being with people he chose to be with, and he was not going to screw this up by talking about it. Mallory gasped into his kiss, and her fingers gripped tightly to his shoulders as she kissed him back as if trying to suck him into her. She was passionate and beautiful, everything Jericho had wanted for his first time. Love was not in the equation for him, and after seeing what happened to his parents, he wasn't sure it ever would be, but he could savor every moment of being in this woman's arms.

When Mallory pulled away, he found himself panting as he moved in to kiss along her skin. He used his mouth to lower the strap of her tank top, wanting to feast on every inch of her body he could reach from the position they were in. The ravenous hunger taking hold in him made him want to never stop tasting her and touching her.

"Jericho, not tonight, not yet," Mallory panted, even as her body continued to roll against his. She was giving him a lot of mixed signals, and it made stopping really hard for Jericho. With how she continued to rub against him, he was sure he would lose his mind if she continued.

"Just let me kiss you a little longer. Let me feel your skin. You are so beautiful, and your skin feels like silk. I can't get enough," Jericho whispered against her ear as he nibbled lightly on the lobe. He let his hands move lower, sliding along her legs and up her skirt until he was holding onto her ass. With the pillar behind her and his hips pinning her front, he didn't have to fully hold her, which allowed him the ability to explore.

"I don't want to stop kissing either, but just kissing. I'm not that type of girl," Mallory added, her fingers sinking into his hair and pulling him tighter to her. He moaned at the sensation of those soft digits massaging his scalp.

"I didn't think you were," Jericho growled, the sound coming out more like an animal than the human he appeared to be. It was apparent the vibrations of such a sound sent shockwaves through Mallory's body, because in that moment she cried out and thrust her hips harder against him.

Growling deeper, Jericho started to purr as he sealed his lips to hers once more and began to rock his hips against her. Even with the clothes acting as a barrier, he could feel the heat of her body, and the sensation of them moving together sent him higher and higher. Her breathing became more frantic, and she moved wildly in his arms. Never had he thought he could have such an impact on a woman before, but here she was melting in his arms. He made no move to strip them down, happy to explore her and experience her just the way they were.

Faster and harder they moved, and Jericho slid his arms behind her to keep the pillar from scratching up her back as they became lost in passion. It was an innocent sort of passion, an almost forbidden pleasure, but it was thrilling nonetheless. Then it happened. Her body began to convulse in his arms, and her back arched deeply as she screamed out into the night. Jericho gave a couple more frantic thrust of his own body before he felt that familiar shiver race over his own flesh, but he held back just enough to keep from embarrassing himself. Instead, he enjoyed the sight of Malloy's orgasm and the pride in knowing that he had given that to her. It was magical and beautiful, and sadly, it was over far too quickly.

Mallory collapsed in his arms, panting and shaking as she came down from her high. Jericho did all he could to hold her and let her recover from the pleasure he had given her until she finally slid from his embrace. "You are incredible. I have trouble believing you have never kissed a girl before. I want to see you again."

He smiled at her words, using his fingers to comb out her hair before petting her cheek. "I really have never touched a girl like this before, and I'm glad you seemed to enjoy it. I'm sure that we can arrange to see each other again. I will be here for a little while."

She kissed him again, and he accepted it like it was the elixir of life. Once they had managed to pull themselves together, they walked back toward the fire and ice chest. Jericho looked around and realized his brother was gone. His heart sank for a moment, but he figured Jax had gotten bored and went to find a place to sleep for the night. It had gotten late during the time he had been with Mallory. Grabbing another beer, he decided it was time to get out of there. Most of the people were either gone or hidden somewhere making out or having sex. It was a good time to walk Mallory home and then find his relief from all the excitement he had just shared.

# Chapter Five

He sat just outside of the circle of people watching his brother with worry and fear. This was an all-around bad idea, and Jericho didn't seem to care. No, he was thinking with his little head and not his big one. Not that Jax could fully blame him; the girl was beautiful and appeared to have an interest in Jericho. She had been all over him from the moment they had picked her up from the diner. Maybe Jax was being too hard on his brother about this. Jericho had a point about needing to have some fun.

Finishing off his beer, he went to get another one. Neither he nor Jericho had ever drunk much, but Jax was large and certain a few beers wouldn't be so difficult to deal with.

"Hey there, why do you keep going and sitting by yourself?" a soft voice said as he leaned down to pull a beer from the cooler.

Standing up straight again, he found Mallory's friend, Desiree, next to him. She was quite a beauty with all those curves and her dark complexion. Jericho could have his little blonde any day. This girl had something more, but Jax would be a hypocrite to act on it. "I'm not very good with people."

"Maybe you just haven't met the right people," Desiree added with a smirk on her face. She held up a flask and shook it around a bit. "Come on, let's have something a little stronger, and you can see if you are at least a Desiree person."

Most of the people who had been there had splintered off. There were sounds of pleasure coming from all over the beach, including where Jericho had gone off to. Jax wasn't so sure he should go with the girl and leave Jericho. What if his brother got in over his head? "I need to stay where my brother can find me."

"Your brother is busy and will be for a bit. Come on, don't be so stiff." She took his hand and led him away from the pier and beach toward a green SUV.

When they got to the truck, he reached out and opened the door for her before going to the other side and getting in. It was a nice size vehicle, and Jax actually felt comfortable in it. "I'm going to have to get something like this one day," he said more to himself than anyone else.

"I don't imagine you fit very comfortably in normal cars. My dad got this for me because he worried I would get hurt on the streets. Now that I'm in college, he wants to make sure I'm okay or whatever. I wouldn't be surprised if there is a tracking device in here." Desiree laughed, moving her seat back, then opening the flask, and taking a swig from it.

Jax stiffened at the idea of there being a tracking device. Running like they were had made him rather paranoid, and he didn't find being tracked a joke. Lost in his worry, he jumped when Desiree thumped him with the flask. Taking the small metal container, he brought it to his nose and sniffed. The alcohol burned at the hairs in his nose, and he shook his head to alleviate some of the sting. "This doesn't smell appealing," Jax said trying to have a drink.

"Get a couple of drinks in you, and you won't care if it smells appealing. It's really strong. After a few shots, you won't feel so stressed out," she giggled and pushed the flask back to him.

Not wanting to come off like a pussy, he lifted the flask and took a quick drink. The liquid inside felt like fire as it traveled down his throat and hit his stomach hard. He gasped, panting from the way it churned and bubbled inside of him. Desiree was laughing as she sat next to him, but when he turned to look at her, he could tell it wasn't from malice. She seemed genuinely friendly toward him, so he let it go and took another shot. The second one was much easier to get down than the first.

Taking the flask back, Desiree took another swallow before passing it back. "I have never seen a guy like you before. You are huge and rugged. It is like you came from some hidden mountain cabin from a hundred years ago."

He had never thought of himself like that, maybe because he never really thought about being human like most people would. He looked the way he did and dressed like he did because he didn't see the point in cleaning himself up to fit some standard in human society. "I did come from the mountains. Where I grew up was outside of a settlement that was established in the 1800s. So, I guess you are right about that. I don't know. I guess I am just me."

"I like it. I find it sexy that you are all natural. So many guys are like your brother all cleaned up and fitting a mold, and you are just you." Her voice got deeper, and Jax turned to look at her just in time for her lips to press against his. He had no idea what to do and ended up pushing her away. "What? I'm sorry, I just like you, and you looked lonely."

"Umm ... I just." He felt bad for pushing her away now that he was more prepared. She was a beautiful girl, but Jax had no knowledge of how to make a girl happy. He had never kissed anyone, held them, or done the things men were supposed to do to please women. Besides, he wouldn't do that to her. Not only was she his boss's daughter, but he knew he would just leave her after a couple of days. "It isn't you. I just don't want to be that guy. You are beautiful and nice. You deserve a guy who will be around, and that isn't me."

"Jax, I'm not looking for Mr. Right. I'm young and in college. I'm looking to have fun. You are the sexiest guy I have ever seen before. I don't care if you are just passing through." Desiree moved in closer and ran her fingers through his beard.

Her body was warm as she climbed over the center console to sit in his lap. What was happening to him? Things like this were supposed to happen to his brother, not him. He was just along for the ride. Once she was settled in his lap, she began to nuzzle up against him much like a cat would, and it made a deep purring sound resonate from deep within him. She felt good. She felt too good, and it was doing nothing for his sanity. He involuntarily slid his hands up her legs to rest on her hips.

"I swear that you are purring. It feels really good," Desiree whispered before moving in to kiss him again. Now that he was expecting it, he did all he could to enjoy it. She tasted like the whiskey they had been sharing, but there was an undertone of sweetness coupled with it. He growled deeply and tried to follow her lead as she deepened the kiss and began to explore his mouth with her tongue.

He didn't know what to say to her. He was purring, and the way she was reacting to him was making him feel things he never had before. His hands slid higher up her body, tracing her curves, and he worried for a moment she would feel how he was responding to her. It took a lot of

60

willpower for him not to crush her against him and ravish her the way his racing mind was demanding.

His deep purr turned into a hungry growl, and all of his words of wisdom to his brother were gone. He lifted her easily, moving her so her knees fell to either side of his hips and making her dress ride high up on her hips. That was when he remembered she hadn't been wearing underwear. Curiosity getting the best of him, he ran his hands down her body and over her nice smooth ass.

"Your hands feel so strong," she whispered against his lips, making him smile.

"I have to be strong to be a mountain man. It is part of life for me," he answered hoping he didn't sound too cheesy. He really shouldn't talk to people. It never worked out well for him.

Desiree ran her tiny hands over him and pulled at his shirt until she managed to get it off him. His breath caught as she looked him over. Why he was nervous, he did not know, but it took him a moment to relax while her eyes got their fill of his body. "You're covered in muscles. A girl could get used to feeling and kissing you."

Not sure what to do, he simply crashed his lips to hers again. He was getting used to this kissing thing, and she seemed to be enjoying it. The thick scent of their arousals filled the confines of the truck, making his head spin with his growing lust for her. Their kisses grew wild, and before he realized what he was doing, he shredded the dress she had been wearing and tossed it to the back seat. Again Desiree laughed, and Jax took the time to move down her body. He kissed her neck and chest. His mouth watered as he took in her beautiful, full breasts, drawing a nipple into his mouth for him to suck upon.

Now Desiree was making the sounds Jax had heard earlier. Her hips rocked against him, grinding into his obvious erection. He groaned loudly, gripping her hips more so he could feel the way she moved. He should stop this. He had told his brother to not get messed up in this sort of thing, but it was so much harder to say no with Desiree all over him. He wanted so badly to finally know what it would feel like to be with a female and not just his hand.

She pulled at his pants, popping open the buckle and sliding down the zipper. More fear and worry that he would botch this whole thing ran through him as she reached into his pants and pulled out the part of him begging to be inside of her. "Do you have a condom?" she asked, and Jax felt his head spin more. Her hand was firmly working up and down his shaft, and she expected him to think?

"I, ummm ... "He wasn't even fully sure what she meant. His parents hadn't talked to them much about sex, and he certainly hadn't been exposed to it. All of his experience with the subject consisted of his own natural urges as he came into puberty and the sight of animals in nature during mating season.

"Don't worry, I have some," she answered flinging open the center console and pulling out a strange square thing. She ripped it open and pulled out what looked like a round piece of plastic. Not wanting the mood to die, Jax went back to tasting her skin while she moved about. He had no idea what she was doing, but she seemed determined on it. The round plastic was placed on the tip of his cock, and she unrolled it to cover his entire shaft. Looking down, it looked like he had been prepared for a rain storm or something. "There, now we can keep going."

Nothing she was doing made sense to him, but he reached down and pulled the lever next to him that pushed the chair back as far as it would go before she lifted her body over him. His breath raced as he watched her, everything happening as if in some sort of fantasy. Then she was on him, and he was inside of her. A roar of pleasure burst from his throat as he arched back. Nothing had ever felt better. She moved effortlessly against him, and it took everything in him to force his eyes open to watch her seductive dance. She was curved back, her hair flying about her naked body. The way she rolled and bounced was erotic and enticing. Leaning in, he began to kiss her more as his hips thrust on their own, giving back to her what she was giving to him.

Their passion grew more heated as they got lost in each other. The windows fogged up, and the truck was rocking hard back and forth. Jax was wild with his desire, and then she screamed out. Her nails dug into his shoulders, and she arched back against the dashboard. He felt her body convulsing against him, and he could no longer hold on. He thrust hard one more time and his own release washed over him, making him roar with the intensity of it all as he shook and writhed in her arms.

It felt like eternity they were locked together in each other's arms, but it was really only a couple of moments. Desiree collapsed on top of him, and he fell back against the reclining chair. They lay there, breathing hard, trying to calm down after the tempest they had just shared. Jax was sure he just made the biggest mistake of his life, but he couldn't bring himself to regret it. Not with the way she shook in his arms and her body gifted him with tremors of remembered pleasure.

# Chapter Six

The truck stop they had gone to earlier for showers was now packed to the brim with truckers parking for the night. It was late, really late, and Jericho was both hungry and horny. As much as he hated to admit it, he had gotten used to the steady flow of release his life of prostitution gave him, and Mallory had left him in desperate need. With Jax nowhere to be found, he figured it would be good for him to try to earn a little money and maybe get some food.

As he prowled around the parking lot trying to not look like he was there to be propositioned, his mind wandered to everything that had happened since they arrived in town. For the first time since their parents' abduction, Jericho wanted to stay for more than a few days. He wanted to make money the honest way, like Jax was going to, and maybe even date Mallory. She may not be his forever girl, but she deserved more from him than a couple of heated nights before he abandoned her for the next town on their endless journey to stay one step ahead of SLICE. She was a sweet girl who deserved more than the life he could give her, but he suddenly had the urge to try anyway.

"Hey, you, come here?" He heard the sound of a man's voice calling from behind him and turned to see who it was. Standing there a man in his mid-thirties. He was dressed in jeans and a T-shirt with a baseball cap on his head, covering a mass of reddish-brown curls. The man was of average height but seemed to really take care of himself, leaving him with smooth muscles.

"Hey, what's up?" Jericho asked, not wanting to come off too obvious in case this guy was just wanting to ask a question or get directions. However, he took his time walking toward him, letting the man get a good look at him. It also allowed Jericho time to really look at the man.

Once they were face to face, he saw the heat in the man's eyes and knew this was what he had been waiting for. "Look, I don't usually do this sort of thing, but umm, my boyfriend left me before I left for this run, and I really just need someone to take my mind off of things. I have a hundred bucks if that will buy me some time."

Jericho was stunned. Most of the men in the past offered around fifty dollars for his time. Looking around for a moment to make sure no one was watching them, he nodded to the man. "Lead the way so we can talk somewhere more private."

The man kept looking around too and then motioned for Jericho to follow him. They walked up to a bright red semi truck and climbed inside. This wasn't the first time Jericho had been in the cab of a truck like this, but this one was much cleaner. Either the man was new to the business or simply liked to keep things tidy. He watched as the man went through the curtain that led to where the bed was and then followed.

"I really don't know how any of this works. I have been with my boyfriend for a really long time, and he just suddenly left me a couple of weeks ago. I heard one of the guys in the diner say they knew who you were and what you do, and it got me thinking. I know it is crazy, but I really just need some mindless sex so I can think straight," the man explained as he went about cleaning the already clean sleeper area, a nervous habit Jericho was sure.

Moving in closer, Jericho could feel the man's nervousness. He reached out and put his hands on his shoulders and waited for him to look up. "Look, we can do whatever you want. You don't have to be so nervous. My name is Christian."

"I'm ... umm." The man bit his lip, and Jericho knew he didn't want to use his real name.

"Just make something up. You don't have to tell me your real name. Tonight, be who you want to be." Jericho encouraged him, running his hands down the man's arms. He was fairly handsome now that they were closer; something Jericho didn't often get from truckers and that the other men who propositioned him.

"Pete, you can call me Pete," he answered, his voice getting soft. Jericho smiled, letting heat fill his eyes. He thought of how everything had gone with Mallory earlier and let that lust fill him as he moved in. This was going to be an interesting encounter, and he had a feeling he would be walking Pete through it all.

\*\*\*

Jax had left his shirt with Desiree so she would have something covering her. Her dress would no longer cover her as it was in tatters, and he didn't want her to get pulled over for being naked. He didn't mind; he was still burning up. With the biggest grin on his face, he went in search of his brother but had no luck finding him. Most everyone was gone, and the few people left moved away from him when he came near. Panic filled him, and he went racing back the way they had come. Jax could think of only a few places in town to look.

The diner was closed, so he was sure Jericho wasn't there. Trying not to look like a mad man, Jax then made his way back toward the truck stop. There were a lot more trucks there now, and people were filling the inside store area. Looking around, Jax hoped he would find his brother here. If he didn't, he wasn't sure where else he would go to look.

Turning the corner from one truck to another, he saw Jericho stepping down from inside of a truck. Another man at the door of it grinned down at him, and both looked disheveled. The panic Jax was feeling was replaced quickly with rage. What the Hell was Jericho doing in that truck with some strange guy? Moving to the shadow, he waited for his brother to come toward him.

That familiar scent was all over his brother as he pulled him into the shadowed area where he was hiding. "What the ... Oh fuck, Jax. You scared the shit out of me."

"What the Hell is going on, Jericho? I want the truth. No more lies," Jax demanded slamming his brother against the front of the truck.

For several long moments, Jericho started at him. Jax could see anger starting to form deep in his brother's eyes, but he could also tell it was a mask. Deep down, there was shame. "I do it for the money. I do it to take care of us, so we can eat and have a place to sleep.

"Damn it, Jericho, I don't need you to take care of me! I'm not a baby; I'm a man and can take care of my damn self! You didn't have to do this! You never had to do this!" Jax exclaimed, fighting his own shame. Part of him had known what his brother was doing, but he had never pushed it enough. "We can make this work without you selling your body and soul to the highest bidder. You are better than this, Jericho."

"No, there have been too many nights where it came down to us starving or me spending twenty minutes letting some guy get off. My pride is not so high that I would let that happen to you ... to us. I am a man too, and this was a choice I made. I could have said no. I could have turned away from it or found something else to do, but this is the choice I made, and there is no going back now." Reaching in his pocket, Jericho pulled out the money he had earned and threw it at Jax before shoving away. "Not everyone is as lucky as you. You don't feel things like I do. I want to be like them, Jax. I want to be normal, have friends and a girlfriend, and do stupid shit. I want to not worry if I fuck some girl that I'm going to get her killed because of what I am. You have the luxury of turning into your beast and wandering in the woods. That makes you happy, but it doesn't make me happy. I wasn't happy before. You know that. I wanted to leave, but I couldn't. Now... now it's too late, and we have no more choices."

Guilt hit Jax like a steel rod to the face. He had given Jericho a lot of grief about Mallory, and all his brother wanted was for a normal night. Instead, his brother had hit the streets working while Jax did exactly what he told his brother not to do. He felt like such an asshole. The worst part was Jericho was right. They would be dead if not for what Jericho had done. "We aren't normal, brother, but you are right. We deserve to be happy. We deserve to have some sort of happiness."

Now that he was calming down from his anger, Jax could see his brother shaking. His eyes kept darting around, refusing to settle on Jax, and that worried him. "Look, it's stupid to fight over this. Let's just go and get a room for the night and something to eat. I just want to go to bed."

Moving toward his brother, he did something he seldom did. He pulled him into him and hugged him. "I'm not ashamed of you. I just worry about you like you do me. I love you, brother, and I'm stupid for the way I have acted today. Come on, let's go and get a place to sleep. I have to be up early in the morning for work.

# Chapter Seven

Morning came early, much earlier than he had wanted, but it didn't matter. Jax was going to help make them some money so his brother wouldn't feel the need to sell himself for the rest of his life. Climbing out of bed, he rummaged through his backpack to find a spare shirt and dressed. Outside the sounds of the beach and the morning sang out, ready to face the day.

Jax was careful to be quiet and not wake Jericho. Once they had both calmed down, he had told his brother what had happened between him and Desiree, and they had been able to rest some. Jericho had teased him lightly, but there was a hint of jealousy in his brother's eyes. Apparently, things had not gone as far for Jericho and Mallory as they had for him. Jax had no doubt his brother would figure out a way to get a second date with his girl though.

As he left the room, the air held a bit of crispness to it as Jax made his way toward the construction site. With how early it was, there were few people about, making the walk peaceful and relaxing. For a moment, Jax thought of stopping to get something for breakfast, but he wasn't hungry, and he would rather save his money to get something for Desiree. After all, he could be a gentleman when he wanted to be. Jericho didn't get all the charm.

Standing by the site was a group of workers, dressed in jeans and old ratty T-shirts, drinking coffee. Jax said nothing as he hunted down the foreman to report for his day of work. The man he had spoken to the day before leaned against a worktable, going over blueprints and marking things as needed. Jax walked over and waited to be addressed.

"Oh yes, Mr. Masterson. I wasn't sure if you would actually show up. I heard word that you spent quite a bit of time out at the pier with some of the other teenagers in town. I thought you might be too tired to actually get out of bed this morning," the foreman said, not really looking up at him. There was a tone in the man's voice that made Jax wonder if he knew what had happened between him and Desiree the night before.

"I promised to be here, so here I am. I don't make promises I can't keep, and I really need the work," Jax answered not wanting any of his insecurities to come through in his voice.

"Yes, well, we shall see. I am going to put you with Charles. He is doing framework over there and could use help with the heavy lifting. I am to be referred to as Mr. Amets, do not call me anything else, are we clear?" the foreman explained, his eyes narrowing on Jax as best as his smaller, shorter frame could muster.

"Yes, sir. Thank you for the opportunity," Jax answered, walking toward the man Mr. Amets had pointed out.

Charles was a short, round man with dark tan skin and a balding head. A cigarette rested between his chapped lips, and a pair of old, wire-framed glasses was perched on the tip of his nose. Jax was sure the man had seen better days. "Ah, fresh meat. I was wondering if Ol' Amets was going to find another temp to suffer through a day with me. Look, I don't mess around. I am here to work and make money. If you want to mess around, then you need another job."

"I came here to work, too. I am not the type to go messing around typically. I don't really have anyone to mess around with," Jax answered.

At the sound of his voice, Charles looked up at him, his eyes growing wide when he realized just how massive Jax was. It wasn't the first time someone reacted that way to him, and Jax said nothing as the man worked to find his composure. He was well aware that his appearance intimidated people. It was why Jericho had been so adamant that he couldn't help make money.

"Right then, let's get to work," Charles chuckled to himself as he began to show Jax what was expected of him.

Even with this being his first job away from home, Jax found that he picked up on everything quickly. He was mostly being used as a pack mule and heavy lifter, which served him well. Throughout the day, he could hear other workers joking around and goofing off, but Jax stuck to the job at hand. Between how both Mr. Amets and Charles reacted to him, he had something to prove and every intention of living up to who he should be.

The shift dragged on for hours, but Jax refused to let it get him down. He knew he would be tired, but he had made the decision to stay out all night. Part of him wondered if Jericho had found a way for all of them to go out again. For the first time in his life, Jax wanted to stay where he could be around people, mostly so he could spend more time with Desiree. Sure, it could have just been a passing curiosity for her. Maybe she was over him now that they had shared the night together, but he was not going to be the one to ditch her. At least not until they were forced to leave town again.

***

Jericho could not shake the feeling of anxiety he felt waiting for his brother to get off of work. It was strange to think that Jax was out with people and Jericho had to stay behind instead of help him work things out. After a pot of coffee, another shower, and pacing the floor for a couple of hours, Jericho couldn't take it anymore and headed for the High Tide to see how Mallory was doing.

A smile spread over his lips thinking of the girl he had spent the evening with. When he had told Jax about everything, he had been shocked to learn Jax had jumped head first into Mallory's friend, or rather dick first. The jealousy wore off over night, and he was happy for his brother, but that didn't mean he was going to give up his pursuit of the girl he wanted. Swinging through the door, he grinned when he saw Mallory's blonde ponytail bouncing behind her as she delivered food to a table of older people dressed in loud Hawaiian shirts. When she turned around, she gave him the most devastating smile. A smile he was sure would bring him to his knees.

"Hey there, Desiree told me Jax is working for her dad today, so I didn't think I would see you until after dinner," she said, grabbing a menu and leading him toward a table. Jericho slid into the booth and smiled up at her.

"He's working, I'm bored. I couldn't take just sitting around, so I decided to come here and get something to eat and see how you were doing," he answered, watching as she slid in across from him. The diner was fairly empty, so he was glad she could sit down with him for a moment or two.

"Oh, I see. He will probably be pretty tired after working on the site all day, I bet he will come home and pass out. Do you think you might want to go do something?" she asked, a light blush rising on her cheeks.

"Aren't I supposed to be the one asking you out?" Jericho chuckled and reached out to take her soft, warm hand.

"Maybe, but I heard that if you don't go after what you want, then you won't get it." The way she smiled at him made his heart stop. Yeah, he really liked this girl.

Shaking his head, he leaned over the table and kissed her cheek. "You might be right about that. So I guess I can pick you up after work again. Maybe we can go on a real date this time. I think it would be nice for it to just be the two of us."

Mallory blushed again as someone called out her name. She jumped from the booth and headed for the kitchen. "I will be back in a second to take your order. Oh, and yeah, I think that would be a great idea!"

Jericho took a moment to watch her before deciding what he wanted for breakfast. The sensation of ice running down his back hit him and he looked up, but nothing was different. Still he couldn't shake the fact that something was off. Someone was there that did not need to know he was in town. No one new had walked into the diner, and there was no one already there who screamed of being part of SLICE, so Jericho did all he could to calm down. There was no point in stressing out over it.

When Mallory came back, she took his order. Being that they never really got to eat, Jericho took advantage of having some extra money and ordered a large breakfast and juice. If something was going to go down, he would need his energy and wits about him. Getting lost in his meal, he nearly jumped when Mallory plopped back down in the seat next to him.

"My boss said I could go early today. I am over on hours and am always working extra shifts. He said it was slow enough and it looked like I had better things to do. So do you want to hit the beach then we can get cleaned up for our date?" Mallory announced, leaning over and kissing his cheek.

Not wanting to miss out on any time with his girl, Jericho quickly accepted. He finished his meal and went to pay for it, but Mallory had managed to get the ticket thrown out. This girl was going to get him fat, and he was pretty sure he would be okay with that. If he didn't have so much to worry with dealing with SLICE, he would happily stick around and see if he could make more with this girl. Something about being with her felt right.

\*\*\*

Jericho lay sprawled out on the beach, watching the emerald waves turn to foam before splashing onto the shore. For the first time in months, he felt at ease and peaceful, like he could actually live the life he had always wanted. Mallory was dancing around in the white waves, giggling as she splashed around. Her body was covered by a small pink and white polka dot bikini, giving Jericho a perfect view of her luscious curves. He smiled as he watched her, thinking he might be able to fall in love with this girl.

He had only just met her, but something about her had him enchanted. She was more than just a pretty girl. She was the type of girl he was certain he could talk to and never get bored. He even believed that one day he could tell her the truth about him, and she wouldn't care.

Getting up, he dusted some of the sand from his body before he went racing toward her. She shrieked in delight as he reached her, lifting her up in his arms before spinning her and falling with her into the ocean. It was a comfortable feeling, one that only cemented more just how much he wanted this to be real.

"Oh my goodness, I can't believe you did that!" Mallory laughed as she came back up from the water. Droplets of the sea rolled down her skin, making his mouth water.

"You have spent the last two days with me, and you can't believe I would find an excuse to pick you up and toss you around?" He gave her a questioning look as he moved in closer to her. His arms wrapped around her, and he kissed the curve of her neck, tasting the salt of the water mixed with her sweet skin.

"I guess you are right, but still." She moved in closer to him, and they kissed deeply, their arms holding their bodies tightly together as they got lost in each other. The waves rocked them back and forth, but he never let her go. The part of the beach they had chosen was away from the tourist attractions, so they had a lot of space to themselves.

When they finally pulled apart to breathe, Jericho cupped her face. Her blue eyes shined up at him with such happiness that it was overwhelming.

"I have never felt like this before," he whispered without thinking. It came out of his mouth faster than he had thought, and he looked down embarrassed that he said something that probably sounded like a pick-up line.

"Me either. Like the first time I saw you was all it took. My mom thinks I'm acting crazy and putting myself in danger, but I don't feel that way with you," she answered, leaning up to kiss him again.

Her words froze him though. Technically she was in danger. Not because he would attack her or hurt her. He would rather die than do anything to hurt her, but she was still in danger because of what he was. If SLICE found him, they would probably want to take her as well. Being with him could very well get her killed.

"Jericho? What is it?" he heard her say as her hand moved his face so they were looking deeply into each other's eyes.

"I'm sorry," he whispered, trying to shake the bad feelings he had been having all day. "I think what happened to my parents keeps coming into my mind, and then I get a bit distracted. Look, Mallory, I don't want you to think I am just feeding you a bunch of lines. I really like you and have no idea how to really express it to you. But I also know that I won't be staying here long. My brother and I are trying to find a way to deal with what happened to our parents, and I'm not sure that is here."

He watched as her sweet and loving face fell to sadness. It was better to tell her now than to wait, but it still tore him up on the inside. If things were different, he would stay. He would play with her on the beach and dance with her at night. He would find a real job and try to find a way to be a normal guy. Unfortunately, normal was not part of his vocabulary. He was a shifter, and she was a human. If she stayed with him, her life would be nothing but chaos.

"Jericho, I ..." She moved in to give him the most heated kiss he had ever had. He might not have had a lot of experience with kissing and dating, but this girl knew how to set his body and soul on fire. If she had been a shifter, he would think she was his soul mate, but being human made that highly unlikely.

They kissed there in the ocean until he could no longer stand it. Her body was shaking against his as the desire for more was growing. He moved her to the deeper water so any random passerby would not see them. The connection between them was far too strong, and he would regret it forever if he did not have her at least once.

She seemed to understand what he was doing and kissed him harder. Her lips then moved down his neck as she hopped up and wrapped her legs around him. The movement of the ocean had them rolling together, and he slowly pushed his shorts down just below his hips. He certainly did not want to risk losing them in the water.

With them locked together, he used one hand to hold her tightly and the other to slide her bikini bottoms to the side, giving him access to her body. She gasped against him but pressed in closer. "I want you, Mallory. I can't get the idea of you out of my head."

"I want you too. I just, I don't usually act like this," she whispered against him. He could feel the opening of her body and wanted so badly to just take her, but he held off for a moment, teasing her so she would be better prepared.

"Trust me, I don't either. There is just something about you," he answered.

They kissed again, and with their lips locked, he thrust into her body, and she cried out into his mouth. A wave of pleasure burst through him, and he shivered at how intense it was, but he had a woman to please, a woman who cared about him for him and not because he was some sort of cheap thrill. He gripped her tightly, rolling her against him as their tongues dueled violently within their mouths. Her hands held tight to his shoulders, and to his surprise, she used her arms and legs to roll her body against him.

Their movements became a tempest of passion as they clung to each other and made love. Never had Jericho thought to feel as powerful as he did in that moment. "Oh fuck, Mallory. I never want this to end."

"No, me either. Please, don't leave, Jericho," she panted against him.

It broke his heart when he heard those words, but there was no stopping. He was too lost in the pleasure they were building between them. Jericho found himself clinging to her, holding her more tightly, and then she was crying out as she crashed her lips against him. She writhed in his embrace, and he nearly collapsed as his own release washed over him. He shook and clung to her as they kissed; such peace and relief washed over him that he nearly wanted to cry.

"Please don't go, Jericho. I know it's crazy, but please don't go."

# Chapter Eight

Jax was ready to pass out by the time he swung open the door to the hotel room. Between staying up all night and working a full day, there was nothing left in him. Looking around, he realized Jericho wasn't there. For a second, he worried something might have happened to his brother, but then he shook it off. Jericho was probably out with the girl he was so infatuated with.

Shrugging off his clothes, he went to shower, hoping the hot water would not only take the dirt and grime but also relax his muscles. He turned the heat on all the way and then stepped under the jets, letting the water soak into his back. It felt good and helped to make him more relaxed from the day. For the most part, everyone left him alone and let him work. It was a good day, just a long one.

He took his time in the shower, but when he started to feel like he would fall asleep, he stepped out. Wrapping a towel around his waist, he started to make his way to the bed, not even caring about brushing his hair. He had almost fallen asleep when he heard a banging at the door. A very animalistic growl rose in this throat, and without bothering to get dressed, he went to the door and flung it open.

"What do you — oh ..." Standing on the other side of the door was Desiree, dressed in a pair of jeans and one of those tiny shirts that showed too much skin. In her hand was a bag full of takeout food. "Sorry, I didn't know it was you."

"It's all right. I heard you worked hard today, so I thought I would make sure you had some dinner before you went to sleep. Charles said you didn't eat anything all day," Desiree answered, making her way into the room.

Jax scrambled to make sure his towel was up around him, covering his body. He had been told walking around naked in front of people, even people you had sex with the night before, was taboo. "I didn't. I was too tired and focused on working."

"Well, are you hungry?" she asked and gave him a heated look. It was the same way she had looked at him the night before, and it made it even more difficult for him to keep his composure.

Moving toward the bathroom, he grabbed a clean pair of pants and slid them on. "Yeah, I am hungry. Thank you. I didn't think to stop for food because I was so tired, but food would probably be good."

He watched her smile as she began to pull boxes of food out of the bag and opened them up. "I brought Chinese takeout. I hope that is okay. I thought it would fill you up well."

Jax breathed in the smell of the food and smiled as he sat down at the table. Desiree made sure everything was open, but didn't make up plates, simply leaving the food open so he could pick and choose. "This looks wonderful. Thank you for this. I feel bad. I should take you on a date or something, but I am really tired."

"I'm not looking for a date. I am looking to spend some time with you. I have been raised around these sites and know how hard you work." She handed him a fork and sat in the other chair. Reaching out, she stabbed a piece of meat with her fork.

Taking a page from her book, he did the same, tasting the different food she had brought. They had only had Chinese food once in the past, so he did not have a lot of experience with it. What Desiree had brought was really sweet and rich. It took him a moment to get used to the taste and how thick it was on his tongue. Meat was not meant to be so sweet.

"Oh, hold on a moment," he said, hopping up from the chair and heading for the door. He left it propped open as he made his way to the drink machine and got two sodas for them. Then he came back and closed up the room again. "Here, I thought you might want something to drink with your meal."

She gave him another of those gorgeous smiles and took the bottle of soda from him. Now that they were sitting there eating together, he had no idea what to say to her. What was someone supposed to say to the girl who had taken his virginity by surprise?

"You are shy, aren't you?" Desiree asked as she continued to eat their meal.

"I am not used to being around people. I just ... we grew up in the mountains, and it was only my brother and my parents. I'm sorry, I don't really know what to say," Jax answered, giving her the best smile he possibly could.

She stared at him for a moment and then her eyes grew wide. "Oh my God! You were a virgin last night? I had no idea."

He couldn't have been more embarrassed than he was in that moment. Because of the heat rising on his cheeks, he was more than thankful for his full beard since he was sure the bright red would be blinding. "It isn't something I thought needed to be announced in that particular moment."

She giggled and moved into him, running her fingers through his hair and beard. He loved that she felt comfortable touching him like that. Suddenly he understood what Jericho had been talking about. With Desiree there giving him such sweet attention, he unexpectedly had the desire to be normal. Leaning in, he got brave and decided to lightly kiss her.

Electricity burst through him as she moved in closer to him, and their kiss deepened. Yeah, he could get used to feeling like this, but he was sure she would never understand the animal living inside of him. Jericho could pull it off a lot better than he could. Even now his skin itched to let the beast out.

Pulling away, he stroked her cheek and looked into the dark pools of her eyes. Then his nerves got the better of him, and he pulled away farther. "Desiree, I like you a lot, but I don't know how long we will be here. I don't feel like it is fair to you to keep doing this with you."

"I've already told you how I feel about all of this. I just enjoy spending time with someone that doesn't act like a drunken asshole all the time." She smiled and walked over to the beds. She looked at the two of them and got a wicked grin. "Okay, so which one is yours?"

\*\*\*

Jericho and Mallory had spent the entire day together, wrapped up in each other's arms. He felt like he was walking around on a cloud, and Mallory seemed like she felt the same way. Once they finished at the beach, they went back to her apartment to get cleaned up before going to dinner and a movie. Jericho had never been to the movies before and found it very enjoyable. Of course, he didn't tell her it was the first time he went.

Now the two of them were walking the street, holding hands and eating ice cream. It was quiet and the wind was blowing. Looking up, Jericho had a feeling it was going to rain. "Do you think we should head back to your apartment or my hotel room?" Jericho asked.

Mallory looked up and seemed to think about his words. "Yeah, we might should head that way. If we wait much longer, we might end up soaking wet. The hotel is closer."

"We were soaking wet earlier. I think that is just part of being out on the beach, right?" Pulling her in more closely, he started to head to the hotel room. Already droplets of rain were starting to fall from the sky.

Through the course of their night, Mallory had told him about her life. She had grown up in a small town near Myrtle Beach but moved because of her love of the ocean. Then she started college and that was where she met Desiree. All of her life, she had worked, and she still felt she had to be her own woman. He had a lot of respect for her and the life she lived.

He told her what he could of his life, but there were lots of holes, and he was sure she could tell he was keeping secrets from her. It wasn't that he didn't want to share, but he didn't know her that well and wasn't sure he could trust her. He wanted to trust her, but it wasn't just his life he had to think about. Jax could die if he told the wrong person the wrong things. Even if he was falling hard for Mallory, he had to wait to see if she was really the one.

When they reached the hotel, he pulled his keycard out and swiped it before shoving the door open. The rain began to pour down just as they stepped inside and stopped. Jax was in the bed with Desiree, and they were wrapped around each other. They seemed to be in the middle of it all but jumped and looked toward them the moment the door slammed. Jax grabbed the blanket, making one of his strange animal noises before rolling to guard Desiree from view.

"Oh, I didn't realize you had company," Jericho chuckled as he watched the two of them scrambling around in bed. He was sure Jax would be pissed from not getting to finish.

Jax made another unintelligible sound as he grabbed his jeans from the floor and began to try to get them on under the blanket. "I didn't realize you were coming back."

"You two need to work out some sort of system for this." Mallory was laughing as well, trying not to look at the couple on the bed as they pulled on their clothes.

Desiree wrapped the sheet around her and went about looking for her clothes. "Yeah, might be a good idea for you to hang a sock or something on the door to let someone know that you're getting it on."

Desiree finished gathering her clothes and went to the bathroom to get dressed. Jax stood up and finished fastening his pants before he turned around toward them. Jericho was still shocked he had interrupted his brother. "Look, I'm sorry, I really didn't know."

"It's all right. Are you guys all right?" Jax asked, trying to look anywhere but at them. Jericho could tell Jax was embarrassed, but he wouldn't say anything.

A few moments later, Desiree came out of the bathroom, dressed once again. She made her way across the room and gave Mallory a big hug before going back to Jax. Seeing her standing next to his brother, Jericho couldn't help but smile at just how much taller he was.

Thunder sounded and the lights flickered for a second. "Looks like we are going to be in for a long night. How about we play cards or something? I have some liquor in my car I can grab, and we can just make a night of it," Desiree suggested walking toward the door.

Jericho and Mallory stepped out of the way, and Mallory cheered in delight before jumping on the bed Jax and Desiree had not previously been in. Jericho couldn't blame his brother for how he felt. He knew having a pretty girl around was a hard thing to say no to. All the same, he still felt like Jax was being a hypocrite.

Jax moved in close to Jericho while the girls went about getting everything ready. Without saying a word, Jericho knew his brother felt in over his head. Jericho had to admit he was worried too. They could both very easily get caught up in women, and that could lead to them getting caught.

"Come on, we will play spades on the bed. Its fun and we can just hang out and get drunk," Mallory laughed, causing Jericho to look toward her. Yeah, he was sure he would not be able to leave her if things continued on much longer. Crawling into the bed, he got ready for them to play their game and enjoy their night.

# Chapter Nine

The ease at which they were able to fall into relationships was frightening. Jax woke up every morning and reported to work, the girls went to school, and Jericho slept after working in the night. He never told the girls what he did for a living. They just assumed he worked for a gas station or something like that. It wasn't exactly the type of discussion Jericho wished to have with Mallory.

In the evenings, they would get together and have dinner. Some nights Mallory and Jericho would go out and leave the hotel room to Jax and Desiree. Jericho could tell Jax was exhausted from working and trying to have a girlfriend, but his brother never complained. It was the closest thing to a normal life they had ever had, and neither of them was willing to let it go.

Jericho was sitting on a bench just down from the High Tide, waiting for Mallory to get off work. He was certain what he felt for her was love. Everything in him craved to be near her and hold her. However, the fear she might run from him if she knew what he was killed him on the inside. She was so sweet and so pure, but humans were afraid of things they could not understand.

The wind blew, and the scent of the salty seawater teased his senses making him smile. They had made love for the first time while playing in the ocean, and he was sure he would always hold a special place in his heart for the water now.

"You are deep in thought," Mallory whispered a moment before her hands slid down his chest, and she leaned over to kiss him from behind. A smile broke out over his lips, and he turned his face to give her a more powerful kiss.

"I am deep in thought. Come here and sit by me. I need to talk to you about something," Jericho answered, taking her hand and guiding her around the bench until she was seated next to him. He wrapped his arm around her shoulder and pulled her close. Mallory always smelled like a combination of fried food and seawater when she got off work.

"Are you going to finally tell me what it is you are keeping from me?" Mallory asked, shocking Jericho to his core. His heart stopped beating, and his breath caught. How had she known? Then again, how had she not known?

Licking his lips, he turned and kissed the top of her forehead. She was smart and beautiful, everything he could ask for in a woman. So why would she not be perceptive? "It isn't that easy, Mal. I love you, but this ... This is a very hard thing for me to talk about."

"Does it have something to do with your parents? You never talk about them," Mallory asked, reaching out to hold his hands, but sitting up straighter so she could look at him.

"Partly, well, mostly. It's just, my brother and I have been running and hiding for so long now that it is hard for us to open up about things to anyone. You and Desiree are the first people we have ever let ourselves get close to, and it's honestly terrifying." Jericho licked his lips, hoping he wasn't about to make the biggest mistake of his life.

"Jericho, whatever it is, just tell me. I love you too, and nothing is going to change that,"

Mallory said frantically. He could tell she was getting worried, and he hated doing that to her.

Taking her hand, he lifted her and started walking away from the busy beach. They had found a spot that was solely theirs away from the rush, and he knew he would need the seclusion to tell her. "It isn't something I can just say. It is something I have to show you. Mallory, you have to promise me you will never tell anyone about this, not even Desiree. I know she is your friend, but right now ... It is up to Jax to tell her."

Mallory nodded as Jericho pulled them into their secret spot. To this point, the boys had both avoided shifting for fear that SLICE could use the outburst of energy to track them, but Mallory deserved to know. She deserved to see who Jericho really was and make her choices accordingly. Moving her to take a seat, Jericho stood back, not really sure how best to go about this.

"This may be a bit shocking to you. I have never told anyone about this before, so I have no idea how to go about doing it. I am just hoping you will understand." The energy from deep within rose up over his skin. He visibly saw

Mallory shake, but he did not stop. His eyes stayed locked to hers as ripples of his power flowed over his skin.

Shifting didn't hurt. It was as if his body simply slid over itself to form a new him, and that is what he did. His legs twisted and shrank, as did his arms. Fur began to cover his body, replacing the clothing he had been wearing. Slowly he fell to the ground, paws where hands and feet once had been. His whole body shook, and within seconds, the man he had been had faded into a sleek black panther. All that remained were his very human electric blue eyes.

Mallory gasped, moving back on the rock she was sitting on and falling onto her butt. "How ... What ... Oh my God, you are a ... Are you going to eat me?"

In this form, Jericho could not speak to her. Slowly he made his way toward her, nuzzling against her and purring calmingly. Even as a giant cat, he did all he could to show his love and affection for her. He could smell her fear, and his own escalated, but he didn't let it show. Then, with tentative hands, she reached out and began to pet him. He moved into that touch, purring more deeply. As she petted him, he shifted back into his human form, ending up nearly lying across her. He looked into her eyes with worry.

"I'm not human, Mallory. I'm a shifter, so is my brother. That is why we don't stay anywhere very long. There are people out there that would rather see us dead than let us roam free. I love you, but I could not keep doing this with you without you knowing who and what I am," Jericho whispered, hoping beyond hope she would not push him away.

For several heartbeats, Mallory did not respond. Jericho pushed himself off her, ready for the worst. At least then they could move on and not have to worry about leaving their women behind. Jericho was the one attached; Jax was just enjoying the sex. Licking his lips, he sat back and started to stand.

"Jericho, I don't know what to say. It isn't like something like this happens every day. I love you, and what you just showed me shouldn't change that. It doesn't change it, but it doesn't make things any less frightening. If you are running from people trying to kill you, and I stay with you, then they could try to kill me." Mallory sat back up straight as she tried to compose herself.

"Yes, that is a risk," he whispered back, too afraid to look at her.

Her soft hand moved and cupped his cheek, turning him so she could see him. "I'm allowed to be frightened and shocked. It is a lot to think about, but I do love you. Do you think we can make this work?"

Jericho released a breath he had not realized he was holding before he leaned in and kissed her with all of his might. His arms circled her, pulling her tight to him, and he lost all control of himself. Nothing else mattered. If Mallory was willing to find a way to stay with him, even knowing the truth, then he would find a way to make it work as well. They kissed like the world would end, and when they pulled apart, they were both panting.

"I think we can make it work. I mean, you might have to be willing to come with me though. I will do everything I can for you. I will take care of you and provide for you, but I can't promise we will always have a home. This is my life, Mallory, but if you want to, I will gladly make you a part of it," he finally answered, running his fingers through her silky blonde hair.

"I need some time to process all of this, but I do want to be there for you. I do want to be with you," she answered, her own voice breathless.

"Take your time. I just am glad that you are not going to push me aside because of this. I love you, and I don't know what I would do if you had hated me because of this." With one more kiss, he helped lift her up from the ground, and they walked back to the hotel to check on things.

*** 

It seemed no matter what he did, Jax could not please Mr. Amets. He was always on time, if not early, he worked nonstop, not even taking a lunch break, and he never complained about anything. But none of it seemed to matter. Mr. Amets treated him like he was the scum of the earth. Of course, part of that could be because Jax was fucking his daughter. It wasn't like it was any big secret.

On several occasions, Desiree had stopped by the site to see her dad and then happened to come over to talk to him. Then there was the night the two of them had been making out in the driveway of her parents' house when her dad walked out and tapped on the car window. There was no doubt he knew what was going on, and Mr. Amets made sure he knew about it.

However, he never told him to get lost, so at least his work ethic was keeping him employed. It just meant he had to work harder and longer to get any sort of approval. The sun was nearly set by the time he made it to the hotel room, and he was more than exhausted. How did normal people handle women and work? Jax was certain he would keel over any day, but at least he would die a happy man and not a caged beast.

Deep inside, he felt the animal in him stir. It had been far too long since he let it loose. Taking a deep breath, he shook off his clothes and let the magic take him. He needed just a moment to feel the animal inside him. Magic washed over him, and his body morphed into that of a large beast. Jericho took on the image of real animals, usually birds and cats of some sort, but Jax's true form, the form he loved most, was not normal. It looked like a mix between a wolf and a large bear with dark, thick hair and massive muscles. Jericho often said the fur felt like his beard, but Jax wasn't sure about that.

Growling and chuffing, he lumbered around the room, stretching out and basking in the feel of his form. As the beast, he could protect anyone from anything, but it also was a frightening sight. Once he had asked his father why he was given such a strange form. It was like nothing that occurred in nature. His father had simply replied that everyone was given different opportunities and challenges in life, and it was up to him or her to decide what they felt about this. It was then Jax decided he was proud to be the beast.

After rolling around on the floor for a bit, he stood up on his hind legs and walked to the wall so he could scratch his back against it. His animal throat groaned out in pleasure before he slid back down to the floor. A knock came to the door, and he turned to it, knowing it was probably his lover. Not wanting to frighten her, he shifted back, covering himself in only a pair of jeans before he went to answer.

Swinging open the door, he was surprised to see a couple of men standing outside. One of them was a large black man in a suit that was a little too small with a gray lab jacket that was a little too big. His head was shaved bald, and he wore a pair of cheap sunglasses. The other man was slimmer, with red curly hair, and dressed in what looked like a police raid uniform. Instantly Jax felt his blood rush and rage start to take over, but he didn't make a move. At least not yet.

"What do you need?" he asked, his voice harsher and more gravelly than usual.

"Yes, we are here to speak to you about a very sensitive subject matter. It seems you and your brother have broken some laws, and we are here to conduct an investigation and bring you in for questioning," the larger man answered. His voice was strange to Jax, holding an accent unfamiliar to him.

"We have done nothing wrong. I work for a living, and we take care of ourselves. Just two guys trying to live life in a hotel room. Can't help it if we are poor," Jax answered, his hand gripping tightly onto the doorframe of the room.

The man who had spoken gave him a sick-looking smile, and more rage flared in Jax. "Oh, I think we both know that isn't true. Your brother is a prostitute, and you have been caught on several occasions engaging in lewd acts on public property. I think it is safe to say that you both will need to come with us."

Jax growled, but the two men were not fazed by it, and when they moved in as if to force him out, Jax flung his arms out, pushing at them to get them away from him. He watched them stumble, and then he kicked them to push them even farther from him. The red-haired man drew out a gun, and the large man laughed as if he was sure he would succeed in capturing him.

Jax let his magic flare just as the red-haired man pointed the gun at him to shoot him. Just as the shot fired, Jax's magic took hold, and he turned into a seagull. Taking to the sky, he flew as hard and fast as he could toward the beach. He needed to find Jericho. They were going to have to leave. It didn't matter any longer about the girls. They were no longer safe where they were.

# Chapter Ten

Something was wrong. He knew it the moment they reached the parking lot of the hotel. The hairs on the back of Jericho's neck stood on end, and his senses went on high alert. It wasn't like him to feel this way, but it seemed to be happening a lot here in Myrtle Beach. As easy as it would be to ignore it, he was starting to think that maybe he should pay more attention to it.

Slowing their movements, he put his arm in front of Mallory to keep her from continuing. His eyes scanned the lot, looking for anyone out of the ordinary. Not that he was sure of whom that would be. It was a hotel after all.

"What's wrong?" Mallory whispered next to him. She shivered and her breathing sped up.

"I don't know. I think that is why this is bothering me. Something is off, though. Come on, let's get to the room and see if Jax is all right. He should be home from work by now," Jericho answered, reaching to hold her hand as they made their way toward the room door.

When they got there, he realized the door was slightly open, just enough for the lock not to engage. Taking a deep breath, he slowly started to push open the door to see what was inside. Fear consumed him. The idea that his brother had been brutally taken in the same fashion as their parents was suddenly all too real for him. He would do anything to keep that from happening, but he hadn't been there to stop it.

Stepping inside, nothing seemed off. The beds were made, and the room was clean. Nothing was out of place from where he had left it earlier in the day. The only difference was Jax's shirt laying over the edge of the bed. Breathing in deeply, he tried to see if he could sense his brother, and the strong scent of magic filled him.

"Jax used his powers here," Jericho said as he began to fill his bag with all of his necessities. There was no way he would spend another night in this hotel. Something was off, and he would not risk losing his brother or his girlfriend to it.

"Jericho, what is going on?" Mallory asked, frantically trying to help him load up the bags. He could see her body visibly shaking, and part of him hated himself for it. He shouldn't have gotten so involved with her. Life with him simply wasn't safe.

"I think SLICE has been here, and I think Jax ran. We have both been so careful to not use our powers, but I can smell the magic in the air as well as the scent of people that I haven't smelled around here before. Something doesn't feel right, and I am not going to risk staying and finding out what it is. You are going to have to make a choice, Mallory, because I have a feeling we are heading out of town." Jericho did his best to explain as he shoved the rest of their belongings in the bag. He would have to hunt Jax down, which was no easy task, even for him.

Mallory didn't answer. Instead, she slung one of the bags over her shoulder and waited for Jericho by the door. He could see the flush on her cheeks and knew she was panicked. She had every right to be. Jericho did the same with his bag and walked over to her. Before he moved to open the door, he gave her the hottest, most passionate kiss he had ever given her. It was the kind of kiss meant to leave no doubt as to how he felt about her.

The sun had set as they walked back out of the hotel room, and twilight had begun to settle over the area. Jericho took another deep breath in and looked around, trying to find a clue as to where his brother might have gone or if the strange scent of unknown men still lingered in the air.

They moved quickly through the parking lot, Jericho keeping every sense he had open. When they reached the end of the walk area, two men stepped out. One was a massive man with ebony skin and a sick-looking smile, and the other man was a lanky redhead. Both held out guns as they moved in closer. Jericho could run. He could change into a bird and fly away, but that would leave Mallory to fend for herself. Now that she was involved with him, she would be just as valuable to them as he was. There was no other choice except for him to fight.

"Mal, get behind me," Jericho demanded as he stepped in front of her to keep the men from having access to his girl. He felt her small hand press against his back and heard the frantic intake of her breath as he got ready to fight. He would be damned if he went out like this.

"Funny, I would have thought your brother would have warned you. Never mind that, though. We can take you, and your brother will simply hunt you down as revenge. It is a win-win for us," the dark man said in a thick British accent. Jericho had no idea who the man was, but he got the feeling this was more than just a job to him.

"You know, I do like to play and have fun more than my brother. Maybe we can just have a dance and sort it out. I'm the sexier one after all," Jericho goaded, refusing to show his fear to the men before him or the woman behind him.

"You are not funny. We aren't here to play games with you. We are here to take you in on the crimes you have committed. Now, we can do this peacefully, or we can create a scene. Either way, you aren't leaving this parking lot," the man added.

The sound of the gun engaging clicked into place, and Jericho knew he had little time to react. He pushed Mallory back farther and spun, kicking out to hit the gun. Magic flowed over his body and claws elongated out of his fingertips. A roar of rage burst forth from his chest, and he lunged toward the men, swiping at them in hopes of injuring them.

Mallory screamed, but Jericho didn't have time to turn back and look at her. The more slender man jumped back at Jericho first, catching him from behind and pulling him back. His arms wrapped tight around Jericho's throat as he tried to drag him down to the ground. Jericho choked, bucking and shaking to try to dislodge the man holding him. The red-haired man did all he could to pull Jericho into the position he wanted him, ignoring the slices of Jericho's claws through the flesh in his arms.

When Jericho looked up, he saw the larger man was holding the gun steadily pointed at him again. With his eyes wide, Jericho did all he could to control the situation, but everything was happening so quickly.

"So the funny boy thinks he can fight. The cat might have claws, but even lions can fall at the end of a gun," the larger man taunted. Jericho saw the tip of the barrel, and for a moment, his heart stopped. He waited to see if the man was going to kill him or if something else would fly out of the gun.

Then Mallory jumped at him. Her much smaller body wrapped around his large mass, and she used all she had to fight him. Jericho watched as the girl he loved was swung around before being shoved off. The larger man kicked at her, trying to get her to leave them alone.

"I see your little girlfriend wants to play too. You sure are all a friendly bunch. Hopefully you will be friendly when you get to our labs," the man said, laughing as Mallory scooted back from him.

Rage filled Jericho, and he flipped the one holding him over his back. He went rolling toward where the large man and Mallory were, and the large man jumped back to keep from getting knocked over. The gun fell to the ground, and out of nowhere, something jumped and tackled the larger man to the ground. Jericho smiled, seeing it was Jax in his beast form.

The two of them rolled around while Jericho went to check on Mallory, but his foot was caught by the red-haired guy, and he fell to the ground. Sliding over the pavement, Jericho used his power to continually shift in order to keep his skin from damaging. Growls and grunts sounded from close by as Jax tore into the other man, tossing him around and slashing and biting at his flesh.

Jericho flipped over just in time to see the dark man grab Mallory. His world seemed to slow as the dark man shoved Mallory in the direction of Jax just as Jax lunged forward to attack again. With claws and fangs bared, Jax landed on the small girl, shredding deep into her body. Jericho screamed out and tried to race forward but the red-haired guy had a vice grip on his ankle.

***

Jax backed away; panic filling him, bursting past his usual animal nature. Blood, so much blood, poured out of the girl's body. In the distance he heard another feminine scream, and he looked to see Desiree standing there. He shifted back to his human form and rushed to the injured girl, lifting her in his arms. Jericho managed to get free of the man holding him and reach them.

"What the fuck?" His brother was in near hysterics as he moved to take Mallory from Jax. The two agents began to drag themselves away, too injured themselves to put up much more of a fight.

"I didn't mean to. I was going for that other guy. I didn't have time to react," Jax answered, knowing his excuse was not enough to make a difference.

Warm blood continued to pour from the girl as she panted and gasped for those last few breaths of air. Jericho sobbed, collapsing to the ground with her still in his arms. Honestly, the agents would have had an easy time catching them if they had not sustained so many injuries themselves.

"Mal, oh God, Mal. This is all my fault. I should have left ..." Jericho began.

Jax couldn't bear to listen and see his brother like this, so he turned back to where Desiree had been. She still stood there, her dark hair blowing in the wind and a look of shock and disgust over her face. Jax made a move to go talk to her, but she immediately took off running.

"Jericho, we need to get out of here. There is nothing we can do, but we need to get out of here," Jax said, knowing it made him sound cold and callous. He was though. His mind was not one of emotions and feelings. Even his short time with Desiree had been more carnal than anything else.

"There has to be something we can do. There has to," Jericho cried, his body rocking back and forth as he held the body of the girl he was sure he loved. Jericho was so different from him, and it was times like this he realized it most.

Mallory gave one last shaking breath, and her arm fell lifeless next to his brother. Jax had slashed her too deeply. There was no way anyone would have been able to survive it, and with that last breath, Jericho gave out a wild scream of pain.

Sirens could be heard in the distance, and Jax forced Jericho away. They had to run. There was no other option for them. If they stayed, they would end up in jail, and SLICE would be able to find them more easily. "Come on, we have to go. Be angry with me all you want, but there is nothing we can do. If we stay here, we will be joining her."

Despite not wanting to put his brother through such pain, he yanked Jericho away and dragged him out of the parking lot. They would fly, they would run, and they would forever be changed by this night.

# Chapter Eleven

Her blood still stained his clothes and body like a sick reminder of the cruel joke life had decided to play on him. He was in love. It was something he had never thought to feel in his life, and he had it with her. Now she was gone, and he had left her dead in the street like a piece of trash.

Anger unlike any he had ever known, stronger even than what he had felt when his parents had been taken, washed over him. They sat in the woods somewhere, having flown for as long as they could. They would need to sleep before they had enough energy to shift and fly more.

Jax sat not far from him, leaning against a tree. Neither of them had spoken to each other since leaving the hotel, but Jericho could feel Jax was hurting. If only his own pain was not getting in the way. Rationally, Jericho knew Jax had not intended to hurt, let alone kill, Mallory. However, rational was not dominant in Jericho's emotions now. All he could see was Jax's claws sinking in and slicing down Mallory's tiny body.

A shiver of agony raced down Jericho's spine as he made his way toward the river they had found. He needed to wash the blood away so he could heal. It was the best thing for him to do. Wash it away, and maybe he could learn to pretend it had never happened. Tears filled his eyes as he sank, clothes and all, into the water. His breath coming slow and deep, he washed and cleaned, doing the best he could to remove all the evidence of his lover.

Snapping twigs and shuffling leaves sounded, and Jericho turned to see his brother moving into the water near him. Anger surged, and he thought about lashing out, but the agony on his brother's face was enough to break his heart. Despite all that had happened, they were bothers and could feel each other's pain. Never would Jericho want Jax to hurt. It was his job to take care of Jax, and the one time Jax had tried to turn it around, it had all gotten fucked up.

Turning to look across the river, Jericho went back to washing, still not speaking. "You don't have to speak to me, but you have to understand that I never mean to hurt her. I never meant for that to happen. I was trying to protect you."

Jericho heard the words of his brother but had no idea what to say in response. His turbulent emotions were at war with his mind. He clenched his fist a couple of times under the water and let out a deep breath. "I know. It's okay. I will be okay."

"No, it's not okay. I know it is not okay. When are you going to stop treating me like an ignorant child? You aren't okay; I'm not okay. For fuck's sake, Jericho, I killed someone. I killed an innocent person, and in the process, screwed things up with you," Jax roared, reaching out and turning Jericho to look at him. "There isn't enough 'I'm sorrys' in the world to make up for what I have done."

Jericho looked up into his brother's eyes and saw the mix of pain, frustration, and regret. Jax had been saying it for months, had even proven that he could be a man, and still Jericho did all he could to protect him. It didn't matter that they were twin brothers. All that mattered to him was keeping his brother safe, because he knew something like this would happen one day. Jax didn't think; he reacted. It was all part of the animal nature deep inside of him. Something

Jericho knew he would never be able to control, no matter how hard he tried.

"I don't treat you like an ignorant child; I treat you like someone who doesn't know how to handle being human. If you did, this wouldn't have happened," Jericho shot back, the iron bars on his composure ripping free.

"This happened because we are wanted men being hunted down, and we were both too stupid to realize we had sat still too long. We put ourselves and those girls at risk, and unfortunately, one of them paid for our mistakes. We shouldn't have stuck around. Don't tell me it is because I am an animal. I am tired of it. I am both, animal and man." Jax's eyes were alight with his own rage. His words hit Jericho like ice water, cooling his own fanatical anger.

They stood there, staring at each other, neither one saying a word. Tension built higher and higher, but they were both too stubborn to back down. The more he thought about it, the more he realized Jax was right. As much as he would always do all he could to take care of his brother and protect him, his brother had become a man, and it wasn't fair for him to treat him any different than he wanted to be treated.

Sighing deeply, Jericho looked up to his brother. "You are right. You are man and animal, just like I am. Nothing can change that, and I do need to stop treating you like you can't do anything." Jericho breathed in and out several times, trying to calm himself, but the memories of Mallory's final moments still plagued his every thought. It was hard for him to think past it, but they would have to move forward. They were hunted men, and they couldn't stay still and let their enemies catch up to them.

Jax nodded to him and they both went back to bathing. It would take time for both of them to come to terms with what happened in Myrtle Beach, but in the end, it was not something they could do anything about. Jericho would need to forgive Jax, and Jax would need to forgive himself so they could move forward. Something told Jericho this was not the end of this life for them. There would be more blood on their hands, both of their hands, before it was all said and done. He only hoped their sanity could hold out for the resolution of the coming conflict.

# Chapter Twelve

She sat, shaking in the chair that had been placed before the large wooden desk. Why she was there, she had yet to figure out, but they had promised to help with the nightmares. The nightmares had gotten out of control. Over and over, she saw Jax changing into that ghastly form, tearing into her as they made love. It was horrific. How could he have kept a secret like that from her for all this time?

Sitting in front of her, with his large arms resting on the desk, was the large man who had tried to stop Jax and his brother. Bandages were still covering the wounds he had taken in the fight, but he didn't seem bothered by them. Donovan Wright appeared completely calm and collected when it came to his work.

"You understand that our training is extensive, and we require a lot from our hunters. You are only an eighteen year old girl. This isn't like joining the army. You will be required to be an assassin not just a soldier," Donovan explained as he looked over her records.

Desiree wanted nothing more than to get her revenge and hunt down those disgusting monsters. They had taken her best friend from her and then left her body in the street to rot, as if Mallory had meant nothing to them. They had used her and then dumped her for their own freedom. It was not something Desiree could sit idly by and let happen.

"I understand what is expected of me, and I plan to be the person you wish me to be. I will work hard and become the best hunter you have ever seen," she answered, confidence filling her voice.

Donovan stared at her for a long time before a smile spread over his lips. "That is what I want to hear. I just took over as head of this department. Usually I do research, but now I am working with the hunters. I look forward to seeing you grow."

He pressed a button, and a tall blond man came into the room. He held a hand out to Desiree and helped her stand. The man was introduced as Andrew, and she was told he would be her trainer. Desiree wasn't sure what she had gotten herself into, but she was certain this was the right path for her. She would become a hunter, and those animals would pay for what they had done to so many innocent humans.

As she reached the door, she turned to look back at Donovan. "You swear you will be able to make the nightmares go away."

"Of course, besides, revenge is the best medicine for pain such as yours. Andrew, why don't you show Miss Amets who we have down in one of the labs. I am sure she will be interested to see how we do things here, and who better to start with than the parents of the very filth she so hates. Mr. and Mrs. Masterson have been subjects of ours for some months now, Desiree. I am sure you will find them more than interesting to look at. When you get your fill, Andrew will start your formal training. Have fun, dear, and remember, this is a new life for you. You have much to learn, but you will get what you want out of it," Donovan answered, and Andrew led her out of the room.

Desiree had no idea what exactly she had become involved in, but she was going find the answers here. Finding out Jax's parents were in the facility she stood in only made her more nervous. She had never thought of herself as a killer, but she would become one if it meant keeping her family safe and avenging her friend's brutal death. The drive inside of her was strong, and she would do anything she could to become the best hunter SLICE had ever seen. One day, she would face Jax and Jericho again, and she would be more than prepared. One day, they would be the ones left bloody on the street.

# Reasons for Lonely

# Chapter One

*September 2, 2005*

Donna was running around the living room, dancing and singing at the top of her lungs as if trying to entertain a crowd of thousands instead of one. To be that young and innocent would be a dream for him. Marris's parents had given birth to Donna late in life, and Marris was already a grown man. It didn't stop him from loving his little sister with all of his heart. To him, having her in his life was a blessing, not an indication his parents were trying to start over now they had a chance to screw things up with him. Looking at it any other way felt like a betrayal to the ones who had raised him, and his parents had been nothing but good to him.

Of course, he could think of better things to do on a Friday night than watch his little sister prance around like the pretty little princess she was. It wasn't like women were going to come hunt him down. If he wanted a date, he would have to find his own. However, he had told his parents they needed a night to themselves, and he had brought the bratling over to his apartment for some fun brother-sister time, which, of course, meant he was being forced to watch Disney movies and play tea party. The sacrifices he made for his family were immeasurable.

"Mar-Mar, I want to watch it again," Donna announced, plopping down on his lap and kissing his face. Donna was a small child with long, rusty brown hair with just enough wave to make it float. She was dressed in a yellow princess dress and a pair of Technicolor knee socks. Her dark brown eyes looked almost like black pools in her face, and Marris had often said one day she would break some poor man's heart.

"We have watched that a million times. Why don't we get a snack, and then I will make you a bubble bath?" Marris suggested, standing with her still in his arms. He squished her body together, bending her in half before extending her again. Repeating the motion, he acted like her body was an accordion he was trying to play.

Giggles and squeals resonated from her, and before they reached the small kitchen, Marris gave up and tossed her up on his shoulder so he could give her feet a proper tickle. "Marris! Stop! I don't like being tickled! Stop!" However, she never ceased laughing.

"All right, all right. What do you want to snack on?" he asked, pulling open his cupboard. Young and single meant Marris had little to choose from, at least when it came to stuff appropriate for children. There was plenty of beer; however, his parents might get upset if he offered that to his six-year-old sister.

"Cookies!" Donna exclaimed, jumping up and down beside him.

"Ummm, I don't have any cookies. Let's see ..." He was starting to think he should have prepared more. Tapping his fingers over and over on the wooden cabinet, he peered inside trying to figure out what would be best.

"Make cookies!" was the next suggestion brought to the table. This girl was determined.

"I don't have the stuff for that," Marris countered, arching a brow at her. Donna gave him a stern look then and nodded down at his fingers. That hard, stubborn look planted deep into her childish features, making her look so much older than she really was. He knew instantly what she was saying without her having to breathe a word. Wiggling his fingers a bit, he grinned back at her. "Using our powers to get what we want is wrong. They are meant to be used only when necessary. Cookies are not necessary."

"Pleeeaaase!" she drawled out, and Marris's heart broke. How could he deny her on the night he swore to make the best for her? Shuffling some stuff around, he found a box of cereal he had forgotten was in his cabinet and pulled it out.

"Okay, but we aren't making a habit of this. I'm serious. Our powers are not a game." Marris poured some of the stale, musty cereal into a bowl and then lifted one of the puffed corn balls out.

Energy tingled down his spine and arm before entering the tiny piece of food. It quivered for a second between his fingers before smoothly turning into a chocolate cookie. Smiling down at his sister, he handed it to her and laughed when she cheered in delight before taking the first bite. "You are the best brother ever!"

He had just reached to grab another kernel of cereal when he heard a hard pounding on his front door. Cocking his head to the side, he moved around the kitchen counter to head toward it. Another loud crashing sound beat against the door, splintering the cheap wood. His heart began to pound, and he turned to see his sister's wide eyes. "Run to the bathroom, lock the door, and don't open it for anyone. Do you hear me? Run and find somewhere to hide."

Donna didn't question anything. She clutched her cookie to her and raced for the bathroom door, shutting it behind her. Marris heard the click of the lock but had no time to be relieved by it as his front door shattered. Several men, dressed in riot gear, came barging in, guns pressed against their shoulders. Instinct took over, and Marris realized he would have to fight or run. With his sister in danger, his options became even more limited. Grabbing a hand full of cereal, he charged his power through it and tossed it toward the men. The once innocent food shifted forms until they became small daggers headed straight for the men. One stabbed deep into the shoulder of one of the men, but the heavy armor all of them were wearing sent the blades clattering to the floor.

"Get him!" a man's voice called out, and guns began to fire. Most of the guns shot darts at him, but some had actual bullets. He feared one would go through the wall or door of the bathroom and get his sister.

Adrenaline pumped like fire through his veins, and he charged the men before him. His tall, strong legs anchored down to the floor for balance, as he gripped the gun one of the men was shooting in the direction of his sister. "Get the fuck out of my house!"

He pushed and fought, but the man was strong, and Marris had been caught off guard. The trigger fired and a moment later a scream sounded from the bathroom. Agony raged inside of him, clouding his judgment, and he elbowed the man in the gut before running toward the door. Another one of the men clotheslined him, sending him flying to the ground. "Check that room over there. I've got this one."

Something stabbed into Marris's shoulder, and the world was quickly becoming hazy. Through blurry vision, he watched as a man dragged Donna from the bathroom by her hair and tossed her on the floor next to him. Blood was pouring from the small child's stomach, soaking her princess dress through. "Bullet got her. She's bleeding pretty bad. What do you want me to do, boss?"

"Kill her. It would be a shame to let the animal suffer like that. She won't be any good to any of us anyway," another man said.

Rage, hot like fire, took hold of him, and there was nothing he could do. Whatever they had shot him with was quickly taking effect. He screamed and begged, but it fell on deaf ears. The man holding his sister lifted her and gathered one of the daggers Marris had made from where it had landed on the floor. Marris got one last look at his sister's deep, dark eyes before the man sliced the blade over her throat. Blood flowed from her neck, and her tiny body went limp. He tried once more to scream, but darkness hit him. The image of his sister bloody before him would haunt him forever.

# Chapter Two

Marris felt heavy and weak as his eyes started to crack open. The ache in his heart was far worse than anything else he had ever felt. Part of him hoped it had all been a nightmare, and maybe he had fallen asleep on the couch watching the princess movie. However, the stench he smelled and the bindings holding down his body told him otherwise. Tears filled his eyes, a mix of agony and wrath, and he was not so weak he wouldn't let them fall. Those bastards had killed his sister in cold blood, and they would pay for it. They had no idea who they were fucking with, but they would soon find out.

Opening his eyes the rest of the way, he looked around to find himself in a very sterile-looking room. The walls were concrete and the floor was white tile. Fluorescent lights burned brightly above him, making the room far too bright for his sensitive eyes. There were no furnishings in the room other than the chair he was seated on, and directly in front of him was the only door. Groggy and sick, he pulled at the ropes strapping him to the chair. His muscles stung at the strain, and he collapsed back.

"I'm going to fucking kill all of you," he moaned, trying to formulate some sort of plan.

"You may think that, but there really isn't much you can do. So you might as well get comfortable. Pull up a chair or something," a woman's voice said, opening the door and walking in.

Marris lifted his head and looked at her. She was a dark woman with caramel-colored skin and black hair. Her eyes were large and black, making him think she had some sort of Indian heritage. However, her voice didn't have the accent to fit. Maybe her family was just from there. Shaking it off, he glared at her, trying to gauge any weakness he could find. Unlike most shifters, Marris's power was weird, and he didn't have a lot to work with. He would have to be smart about what he did. "No, ma'am, I don't think. I know I am going to get out of here, and I'm going to kill every fucking one of you."

"How do you presume to do that?" the woman asked, standing only a few feet in front of him. Her legs were set shoulder length apart, and her hands rested on her hips. He could tell she was a strong woman too, her muscles making her clothes tighter than they should be. Fucking Hell, he was out of practice and didn't particularly like fighting women, being a gentleman and all.

"If I tell you my plans, then you could prepare for them. Doesn't sound like a very smart thing for me to do. Do you think I'm stupid?" Marris answered, slowly coming more into his wakefulness.

She chuckled and shook her head. "It says here you turned a handful of cereal into daggers." She pulled one of the knives from her pocket. Blood still stained the blade and rage flared inside of him. Images of his sister's final moments flashed through his mind, and he lunged toward her, falling to the floor. "You want to tell me how you are capable of doing that? We have never found one of your kind who could do that. Most of you just turn into animals."

"Fuck you. I'm going to rip you to shreds, you sadistic bitch!" All thoughts of being polite had left him. The only thought going through him was the brutal slaughter of anyone he came into contact getting out of this place.

"Feisty aren't you. Well, you won't be for long. I'll give you some time to calm down, and I will be back." The woman turned to leave the room, and Marris saw his opportunity.

Magic surged over him and the ropes binding him turned to silk. He flexed his arms, ripping the fabric away from him before gathering it into his hands. Pushing himself from the ground, he took a couple of steps in her direction before tossing the silk toward her. More magic rippled through it, and the soft fabric transformed into a sharp bladed whip. The barbs on the end slashed through her clothing and deep into the flesh of her back. He wasn't really proficient with a whip, but he hoped it would knock her down. The woman shrieked in pain as she fell to the ground. As he pulled the whip back, blood splattered everywhere.

Marris rushed forward, kicking the woman as he passed and slammed through the open door. More people dressed in the same sort of armor as the ones who captured him came rushing to recapture him. The hall was narrow, and he had

144

no idea where he was going, but he knew he would have to fight his way out. Something told him that staying here would be a fate worse than death.

Once more, he used his magic to shift the item in his hand. He turned it into a sword, figuring he would have a little better control over it than a whip, and then charged toward the guards. His violent rage kept him from holding back in any way. These people had killed his sister, and he would show them no mercy. He fought like a berserker, slicing, punching, and kicking, until the hall was littered with bloodied bodies. There was no room in his mind for rational thought, only instinct. When he reached the door leading to the outside, he heard the woman from the room scream after him. "You can run, but you will never hide. We will find you, and we will take you down!"

Outside of the building was a fence lined with barbed wire. It seemed like this building was a makeshift setup, because there were not a lot of people around or protections set up. Men started to rush toward him, but with the amount of adrenaline coursing through his veins, there was no way they would be able to stop him. He charged the fence and began to climb. Gunshots fired behind him, but he was deaf and blind to anything but his goal. Once he was free from all of this, he would be able to think again.

Gripping between a couple of the barbs, he turned the barbed wire into sand before moving to the other side of the fence. He climbed down just enough to not injure himself by jumping, and he pushed off the fence. The guards had reached the gate by the time he landed, but he still had a lead on them. Wasting no time, he turned and ran with all of his might. His muscles burned at the exertion, but he paid it no attention. He could fight through this. He would survive this.

He ran until he reached a road, and then he ran along the road. Finally a semi truck pulled over and offered him a ride. He was reluctant at first but figured it was his best bet. Climbing on board, he told the driver to take him as far as he could. Marris had no money, no belongings, and now was running from someone he didn't even know. How had all this happened? With his heart racing, he tried to find something that made sense to him, but nothing did.

# Chapter Three

*April 2006*

*"How could you? Why did you let them do this to me, Mar-Mar?"*

The haunting sound of his sister's voice woke him from yet another nightmare. Sleep was a fantasy to him at this point. Months had gone by, and he was still no closer to finding out who had attacked him or why. The more time went by, the more the nightmares came. His powers were growing weak from lack of rest, and his body wasn't doing much better.

Sitting up, he looked around him to try to figure out where he was. He had been traveling so much that all the places were starting to look the same. Travel, sleep, travel, sleep was like a mantra to him. Blinking a few times, he saw he was in some sort of underground sewer or subway. He had traveled northeast for a while, but even he wasn't certain exactly where he had ended up. Taking a moment to stretch, he stood and dusted himself off.

Right after breaking away from his captors, he had tried to find his parents, but he had been unable to reach them. He knew going to them would probably end up with him getting caught again. Later he found out his parents had been taken as well. Nothing he found anywhere told him if his parents were dead or alive or who had taken them. Slowly he was starting to lose hope.

"Hey, you, got a light?" someone with a deep, gravelly voice said, calling out to him. He patted his pocket and then pulled out the lighter he had stolen from a gas station the other day. He didn't smoke, but having a way to make a fire was always good.

"Yeah, man, here you go," Marris answered.

The man walked over, took the lighter, lit a cigarette, and took a deep drag from it. "Thank you. You look like you have been running for a while. You know you can't run forever, right?"

Marris felt his blood grow cold. He remembered how the woman had said that to him, and it freaked him out. Taking a step back, he didn't even try to retrieve his lighter. He could always get another one. "Look, I'm just homeless and trying to find a place to settle. I don't want any sort of trouble."

The man looked up at him then with hard eyes. He was an older man with thick gray hair and faded hazel eyes. His beard had grown out and gotten shabby, and his clothes were a mess. Until he had spoken to him, Marris had assumed he was just another homeless man. "Son, I don't want to hurt you. I know what you are going through, and I know why you are doing it. They got to you and your family, didn't they?"

His heart began to race more, and he took another step back. This man seemed to know way too much about his life, and more panic followed suit with it. "What are you talking about? Look, I need to go. Keep the lighter."

"You're a shifter, boy. I know you are. And I want to help you. You had people come after you, that's why you are running." The stranger took another long pull from the cigarette before flicking away some of the ashes.

"How do you know about all of this? Who are you?" Marris asked, finding himself back against a cement pillar. He could run, but part of him was curious what the man would say.

"I know because I'm a shifter, too. I know because they came after me and mine, and now I spend all my time running. You aren't the only one, but if you don't know who they are, they will find you again. You need to know what to look for and how to fight them," the man explained moving closer so he could talk more quietly. "Our world isn't safe, and we have to fight."

Fight? Marris had killed people trying to escape whoever it was trying to capture him. Now he was being told he would have to fight more. Life was really starting to nosedive into the pits. "Who are you, and who are they?"

"They are SLICE, Supernatural Laboratories for the Investigation of Chaotic Entities. Their whole purpose is to hunt down people like us and use us in their experiments. I have heard horrible things about what happens inside one of their labs. Most don't survive it, and I have only met one or two who have been able to escape. I am John. Who are you?" John reached his hand out to shake with him.

"You mean these people are for real? What am I supposed to do?" Marris wasn't even sure he was speaking to the stranger anymore. His head began to spin with all the thoughts wandering through his head. He had grown up ignorant of anything like this. Sure, his parents had told him to keep his powers a secret, but they had never mentioned anything about a group of people Hell bent on hunting them down.

"Kid, there are a lot of things out there people would be horrified to know about. These people, SLICE, they have ways of finding us. Ways I have yet to figure out. But there are others like us who fight back. You can spend your whole life running, or you can fight back. That is your choice." John's face was hard and serious.

"I don't understand. I feel like there is this whole world I never knew anything about. How could this have been going on and without me knowing?" Marris felt his frustration rising as the questions left his mouth. Anger and fear twisted to make his head spin even more.

"There are a lot of things out there you know nothing about. Now you do. What are you going to do about it?" John scratched away at his

151

beard then nodded to an opening in the wall. "Come on, I will fill you in. You have a lot to learn after all."

Marris was shocked. Watching John walk toward the opening, he couldn't help but follow him. If this man knew about the people who had captured him and killed Donna, then he wanted to know all he could about them. One day, he would take them down, but first, he had a lot to learn.

# Chapter Four

*September 2, 2010*

Five years had passed, and still the pain was unimaginable and the nightmares plagued him every night. He could hear her screams and pleas for him to help her, all the while he was forced to watch her be slaughtered. Many nights he would wake with the feeling he was covered in her blood, only it was sweat. Nothing made the pain or memories ease up, but today he would get his revenge.

He had spent the last four years learning all he could about SLICE. Hours, days, weeks were spent hunting them down and tracking their locations. More than that, he had found the woman who had held him captive. Apparently, of all the people he had killed that day, she had not been one of them. He would not be so careless this time around. Yes, today he would finally get his vengeance. The dagger the bitch had shown him, the one used to kill his sister, was sheathed in his pocket. It had been a constant reminder to him of why he was choosing to fight.

"Donna, today I lay your soul to rest," he whispered, fingering the handle of the dagger.

*This will not help you, Mar-Mar. You are doing this for you.* The sound of his sister's voice always haunted his mind. Today, he was choosing not to listen to it. He knew he had to do this, or his sister would never have rest.

He had timed the guard duty and knew they would be passing by shortly. Once they did, he would have a sliver of time to get across the yard and into the building. There were two rotating cameras he would need to dodge as well, and he had been carefully watching them to make sure he would be able to go through without being spotted.

Keeping his breath steady, he crouched low and kept his eyes locked to the perimeter path. The sound of people approaching echoed from just out of sight. Pressing down, tighter to the ground, he watched as the guards moved past. Giving it a few minutes for the guards to get out of range, Marris then began to ease down the hill toward the fence. His eyes kept a close watch on the cameras, and he dodged behind trees whenever it shifted in his direction.

It only took a few moments for him to reach the fence. His fingers laced into the chain link, and he shifted the fence into a gate. Slipping through, he shifted it back before dashing behind a gas tank. His breath came heavy as he waited for the camera to make its sweep. Once he had his opening, he raced toward the building. With both hands outstretched, he turned the wall to a curtain and burst through before returning it to its former shape.

Beyond the wall, he found himself in a dark room. Reaching up, he scratched at his beard while letting his eyes adjust to the darkness. He had lucked out by not rushing into a group of people or a toilet or something. As the room came into focus, he saw he was in a small office. There was nothing special in the office to signify it belonged to someone important. There were, however, a couple of files on the desk. Curiosity getting the best of him as he caught his breath, he decided to thumb through the folders.

The top folder discussed people by the names of Jax and Jericho Masterson. From what Marris could gather, they were twins whose parents had been captured recently in Tennessee. The boys had escaped in the struggle, and their parents had been taken to a base in Oak Ridge, Tennessee. The next file contained information about a young lady named Ashlynn Porterfield. All the information about her sounded impossible. The things she could shift into and the speed they projected she could do it in was insane. How would anyone be able to keep up with her?

"What the fuck?" he whispered.

A sound echoed from the other side of the door, and Marris jumped behind the desk, hoping no one came into the room. A few moments passed, and he realized he was safe. With his mind snapping back into his mission, he set the files down so he could exit the room. With how informative the files were and useful they could be to his people, he had a bitch to kill.

Slowly he opened the door, shifting his clothes to look like a standard guard's uniform. He held himself confidently, not wanting to look as if he didn't belong. Marching down the hall, he looked around for the stairs that would lead to the dumb bitch's office. Through his investigation, he had discovered her name was Nisha Moore, and she had been working for SLICE for more than ten years. That record would end tonight, and he hoped she regretted ever choosing to work for such assholes.

In the name of science and advancing the human race, SLICE kidnapped, tortured, and killed shifters, hoping to find ways to harness their powers. They had the whole philosophy of "If I can't have it, no one can." Science could go fuck itself, because they were hurting and killing innocent people in the process. It was enough to make him sick, and part of what led him down this ruthless path.

Taking the stairs two at a time, his heart started to race with anticipation. The blood on his hands from the escape was a reaction, self-defense, but this would be cold blood. The kind of blood that left stains on your soul. He could feel the weight of it in every fiber of his being. Reaching the top landing, he had to take a deep breath to build up his resolve.

His footsteps echoed like his heartbeat as he made his final path toward his target. Everything he had been building up to led to this moment. At the end of the hall was a door with her name embossed in bronze and black lettering across a plate. It all looked so official and proper.

Reaching out, he turned the knob, and with one last breath, he pushed open the door.

Standing behind the desk, the woman hadn't appeared to age at all. Her black hair hung to her shoulders, and a dark blue suit covered her body. She looked up from a file she was reading when he walked in, and she slowly started to close it.

"Can I help you?" she asked with a confused look on her face.

"No, I think you have done enough," Marris answered, using his power to change the doorknob into a solid mass of steel. He didn't want anyone to be able to open the door while he was in there.

Throwing the folders to the desk, she moved around to approach him. An alarm sounded on her desk, and her eyes squinted. "Oh, I remember you. You are the shifter who can shape-shift objects. You fucked up my back the last time I saw you." Anger filled the woman's voice as she marched toward him.

"Glad to know I made an impression. It had been my full intent. I never forgot about you either, or what you and your friends did to my family," Marris growled, moving toward her as well.

"You can't kill me. You can't do anything to me. I'm going to take you, and you will never get away," the woman said, reaching for a gun holstered on her hip.

Marris took it for the challenge it was and lunged forward toward her. He grabbed her by the neck and slammed her against the desk. His other hand reached and pulled her gun out so she couldn't get a hold of it. She was not going to get a chance to attack him first. He tossed the gun to the side, then reached into his pocket, and pulled out the dagger. It was rusty and dirty, having never been cleaned. He wanted her to see the blood on it and know what was coming. "You and your people hunted me down and killed my little sister. She was only six year old. Six fucking years old!"

"You are an abomination that deserves to be locked away, and that girl was too. She deserved what she got. We put her out of her misery," she spat out, trying to push him off of her.

"She was a little girl! She didn't deserve anything. Neither did I for that matter. We lived our lives and didn't do shit to any of you. Fuck you and what you think." Marris had never felt such rage before in his life. His entire body shook as he pressed the knife against the woman's throat.

"Your kind knows nothing but how to hurt the people around you. You are filth the world needs to be stripped of," Nisha gasped, extending her neck to keep the blade from cutting her.

"No, you are the filth. Until now, I have never hurt anyone, at least not someone who didn't hurt me first. This blood is your doing. I hope you burn in Hell for what you have done." A strange calm came over his words a moment before he sliced deep into her throat. Blood flowed fast, and Marris stepped back to avoid getting covered in it. Flashes of his sister's throat doing the same thing shot through his brain, and he shivered at the memory.

He stood there watching as the woman bled out, her eyes begging for him to help her. That strange cold feeling kept his face hard as he moved forward. So much time, so many hours spent preparing for this moment, and it was finished so quickly. Once the light left Nisha's eyes, Marris took a step forward, staying just outside of the range of her blood. He held the dagger out and used his power, transforming it back into a kernel of cereal and setting it on the desk. A drop of blood fell next to it from where it still coated his hand.

His revenge was over, but his duty had just begun. He was going to help his people find peace and freedom if it killed him. Word had gotten around about groups of shifters were starting to pull together for the common good of their people, and he planned to be a part of it.

# Chapter Five

*December, 2011*

The bell rang as he entered the small diner just outside of Keeseville, New York. It was freezing out, and a blizzard had moved in, covering the area in snow. Once inside of the diner, the difference in temperature was striking. It made Marris stagger a bit and catch his breath as heat overwhelmed him. Shaking his head, he shrugged off his coat and made his way to a booth near the back. He was nervous about this meeting, but it was going to be a good one as well.

There were only a couple of people in the diner, older gentlemen drinking coffee and talking about a time long forgotten. Marris had heard men like them before and had always wondered if he would ever be like them. Would he ever get to sit back and talk to his friends for hours about nothing? The likelihood was slim.

A portly waitress walked over to him to take his order, and Marris smiled up at her. She had a frizzy mess of gray and blonde hair, and her eyes looked old and tired. However, when she got to his table, she gave him a huge smile, "What can I get for you, sweetie?"

He didn't have much money, and he always hated doing this, but he had to survive somehow. Reaching into his pocket, he turned an old piece of paper into a five-dollar bill and handed it to the lady. "Just some black coffee and toast please. I'm just passing through."

"Coming right up, sugar. Let me know if there is anything else I can get for you," the woman answered, taking the five and going to get his coffee.

The door opened and the bell dinged again, a swirl of snow following the person through the door. A tingle washed down Marris's spine as he watched a tall blonde woman enter the diner. She was beautiful, tall, with long legs and gentle curves. Even with the large coat covering her, Marris could tell her body was amazing, and it made a very primal part of him come to life instantly. The woman looked over the room for several moments before turning toward him.

"Marris Stratford?" the woman asked, arching a brow as she stood over his table.

His heart began to beat faster as he looked up at the woman. The energy rolling off her skin was unlike anything he had ever felt before. It was strong, powerful, and wild. There was no doubt in his mind that she was capable of doing many things. "Ashlynn Porterfield?"

A soft smile crossed over those perfect red lips, and she moved to slide into the booth with him. "You look just like I had heard. I'm glad to finally meet you. John told me a lot about you."

"John never spoke of you, but then again, I guess getting information about you out of anyone is difficult. You are not an easy woman to find, Ashlynn," Marris answered, leaning back in his seat.

The waitress brought over his toast and coffee and then asked if Ashlynn would want anything. She declined, and the waitress went back to the counter. "I have to be hard to find. The bounty on my head is too high, and I can't afford to get caught. John tells me you are up for helping free our people and taking down SLICE."

Marris wasn't really sure how John and Ashlynn got into contact with each other. It all seemed rather strange to him that people who did not have phones or permanent residences had some sort of network of contacting each other. "Yeah, I do. They attacked my family, killed my sister."

"I'm sorry to hear that. I haven't met one of us who hasn't suffered such pain. It is crazy just how cruel and heartless SLICE can be. They speak of doing this for the betterment of humanity, but their methods are anything but humane," Ashlynn explained as she twisted and pulled at a napkin. Marris picked up on the nervous energy quickly and relaxed. She might look and sound confident, but deep inside was a frightened girl wanting peace. It was something he could relate to.

"Yeah, I'm starting to realize that, too. It is like they don't care about anyone or anything but themselves. I have met a lot of people lately, and all of them say the same thing. They have been hurt by SLICE. Lives are being uprooted and torn apart, and for what?" Marris agreed, taking a sip from his coffee. The bitter, hot liquid made his throat feel good and warmed his body.

"That is the question. No one really knows why SLICE does what they do. I haven't been able to find a lot of information on their origins. John has told me a lot, but even he only knows so much. It is like they sprung out of nowhere one day and started killing all of us off. But, it isn't our job to figure out why they are doing it. It is our job to stop them." Ashlynn's eyes turned dark and cold as she continued to play with the napkin. There was history there, as Marris was sure there would be for anyone who had found themselves in their shoes.

"Do you know anything about Jax and Jericho Masterson? I saw a file on them when I broke into one of the facilities a year or so ago. SLICE seemed pretty interested in them," Marris continued.

Ashlynn looked at him, her face wrinkling in confusion for a moment. "You broke into a SLICE facility?" The shock in her voice made Marris smile.

"Yeah, it wasn't that hard." Marris chuckled, leaning in closer to her.

"Do you realize how valuable that would be? One of the things we have never been able to do was penetrate their walls. They have a lot of guards and a lot of weapons. How did you do it?" Ashlynn asked in wonder.

"Determination mostly. I also don't have to worry about doors. If there isn't one where I need to go, I make one. John told you about me, didn't he?" Marris answered.

"He told me you were special, but he didn't go into a lot of detail. It isn't John's way to go around telling the secrets of others. Why are you so special, and what do you mean you just make doors?" Ashlynn's curiosity was making her bounce in her seat.

Looking around to make sure no one was watching, he took a napkin from the dispenser and let his magic flow into it. When he was done, the napkin had turned into a pen. Something small and easy to overlook, but the magic was there all the same. He watched Ashlynn's eyes widen and smiled. "I can't change what I look like or turn into an animal, but I can change objects around me. It is just who I am."

"That is incredible," Ashlynn's words came out breathy as she reached out and took the pen. She scribbled a bit on the napkin, seeing it worked, and then smiled up at him. Marris couldn't stop the grin on his face. "I never knew there were people like you out there."

"My sister was the only other one I knew, but she hadn't really developed her abilities. She could only do little things, and they had to be related in a way. Like she could turn a square block into a round block," Marris answered. "Though to be fair, I haven't met many of our kind. Seems to me, we all like to stay spread out."

"We sort of have to. I mean, if we stay still too long or get in larger groups, SLICE finds us. It is a sad state of affairs. Look, we have ways of keeping in touch, but we have to keep it secret and hard to discover. There are places you can get information or messages from me, and we can organize meetings," Ashlynn began to explain. There were a handful of websites, mostly sites meant for buying and selling items, where messages were left. There was a bit of code in it, and she explained what all of it meant so he would better be able to communicate. "The key thing to remember is there will be a place and a color. The color represents what it is about and the place tells you where to go. I won't ever leave details; all of our plans are discussed in person. I can't risk us getting caught."

"That makes sense. Look, I want to be involved. I want to help. I know you got thrust into this life just as quickly as I did. It sucks to be in our situation, but if we can really do this, if we can stop SLICE and give our people a sense of happiness and peace, then it will be worth it. I can't bring my sister back, but I can help others not lose the family they care so much about," Marris added, drinking the last of his coffee.

"It is the whole reason I still fight. We need more people like you, Marris, and I'm glad you are going to help me. So many of our kind are too afraid to do anything. It sucks that it takes something bad happening to one of us to push us to do the right thing. I know that isn't what you did, but you have to admit, it is a driving force. One day, maybe we can get support before the bad stuff happens." Ashlynn pocketed the pen he had made and stood to leave. "I will be in touch. Take care of yourself and keep in touch."

"Same to you, and stay warm. It's cold out there." Marris sat back and watched her leave. The waitress brought him some more coffee, and he decided to enjoy it. It wasn't like he was in a rush to get anywhere, and the snow did not look fun to walk through.

# Chapter Six

*September 2013*

Marris took the stairs leading to the apartment he had been given the address to. Ashlynn had asked him to go and talk to this girl about joining their cause. She was supposed to be smart, fast, and willing to fight. However, she was also gun shy. The litter on the steps and the thick stench of ammonia spoke volumes for how much the woman was trying to hide. Not that he could blame her. Word had gotten out that she had been attacked at work, being forced to flee for her life.

Echoing from down the hall were the sounds of people arguing and the muffled moans of fucking. Yeah, the ghetto was alive and well. Reaching the door he had been told to go to, Marris lifted his hand and gave a firm knock. A gasp followed by whispered instructions could be heard from the other side, followed by careful footsteps. "Who is it?"

"I'm here about the red crock pot." Marris always felt silly with their code, but it was important to keep SLICE off of their trails.

More shuffling was followed by the clicking of a lock. A moment later, the door opened to reveal a petite woman with jet-black hair and bright green eyes. Her skin had a light olive color to it. She only stood to chest height on him and had very slight curves, but she was stunning. For a moment, all Marris could do was stand there and stare at her. "Come on in. The crock pot is over there."

Snapping out of his entrancement, Marris stepped into the apartment and looked around. There was only a couch and small table in the room. Nothing else was in the apartment. Only a couple of backpacks sat open under a windowsill, the sleeve of a pink sweater hanging out of one of them. "My name is Marris. Ashlynn sent me to come and get you. She said you needed safe transport to one of our safe havens."

"I have to say, I didn't think I would actually be able to get any help. I just didn't know where else to turn. I can't do this alone," the woman answered, her body and words shaking. "My name is Ira, Ira Connor."

"Well, Ira, I'm going to make sure you make it safe. Get your stuff and we can get out of here.

172

My truck is downstairs waiting for us. We have a safe house for you," Marris explained, moving over to the bags so he could help hold them.

"Hold on, it isn't that simple. It isn't just me. I have a daughter," Ira explained, moving to a door off to the side. She opened the door and a small girl came walking out with the same black hair and green eyes. The only difference was her skin was much paler.

Marris froze seeing the little girl. Memories flashed through his mind of his sister and how that night had gone down. He had to breathe for several seconds before he composed himself. Ashlynn hadn't mentioned a daughter, and it made him wonder if she had even known about the girl. "Look, I know I didn't say anything about her, but I was afraid. I couldn't risk something happening to her. We have been through so much already."

"No, I get it, but we should have been told. I will have to get word to Ashlynn about this, but first, let's get going. It is even more important we get out of here since there is a child involved," Marris said.

He and Ira shoved clothing and other things in the bags before heading for the door. Ira held the little girl and Marris held the bags. Making sure the hall was clear, they raced down the stairs toward his old blue Chevy truck. Marris was good at making sure he wasn't followed, but even he was not perfect. Once in the truck, he sped out quickly, wanting to get on the road as soon as possible. "Mommy, where are we going, and who is this man?"

"This is Marris, and he is taking us some place safe," Ira answered.

"It is nice to meet you, little one. I promise I am not going to let anything bad happen to you. Are you two hungry?" he asked, looking over to the two of them for a second before putting his eyes back on the road. The little girl gave her mother a look that spoke volumes, but neither of them answered his question. Not waiting for an answer, he pulled into a hamburger joint and made his way to the drive through. "I know the two of you are hungry. What do you want? I can't have you hungry and hurting in my truck. It wouldn't be very gentlemanly of me."

"Bethany, what do you want, baby?" Ira asked in a way to let her daughter know it was okay.

"Chicken nuggets!" the girl answered excitedly. She was all but bouncing in the seat as Marris pulled around to the order screen.

"Ah, a girl after my own heart. I love chicken nuggets. What about you, Ira?" Marris asked, giving the small girl a wide smile. He felt twenty again, sitting with his sister in his old bachelor pad. It was at the same time wonderful and heart breaking.

"Just whatever sandwich they have on sale. I'm not picky," Ira answered in a soft voice. Marris understood how she was feeling. She had been through a lot, and now she was being forced to trust a man she had just met.

"Sure thing," Marris answered before turning to the order box and calling out what everyone wanted. He even picked up a couple of apple pies, figuring the girls could use a treat.

When they had their order in hand, they headed down the road. Over the last couple of years, Marris had been helping Ashlynn set up safe houses all over the country. Whenever one of the their kind found themselves in trouble, Marris, or one of the others working with Ashlynn, would find them and take them to the safe house. Marris had even been known to break into a few SLICE prisons and extract people from the confines. He seemed to have a way of getting around which others did not. It had made a huge difference in their cause.

They were quick to head out of town and toward the safe house. The whole way, Bethany went on and on about different things. She was such a smart little girl who knew a lot about science and nature. Every time they passed a strange tree or animal, she told them what it was and what made it special. Marris was impressed, and the more he was around her, the more she reminded him of his sister.

"I'm sorry, she is a bit of a talker," Ira said in apology when Bethany had finally passed out from exhaustion. The small girl had her head resting in Ira's lap, breathing softly in her sleep.

"It doesn't bother me. My little sister was that way. She always had something to say,"

Marris explained, turning down a dark country road.

"Was that why?" Her words came out like a question, and pain stabbed straight to Marris's core.

"Yeah, it was. She was killed a few years ago. She was only six, and SLICE came in and slit her throat right in front of me. They slaughtered her like a damn pig or something." Anger bled into his words quickly, and he gripped the steering wheel as he continued to drive.

"I'm sorry. So she is the reason you do what you do," Ira said, tears filling her voice.

"It's part of the reason. I just never felt like I could make up for what happened to her. I was babysitting her and should have protected her, but I didn't know back then what I know now. If I had, maybe she would still be here." His tears had dried up long ago, but nothing could take the cold steel out of his voice when he spoke about Donna.

"Don't beat yourself up over that. It isn't your fault, and you couldn't have known. I couldn't imagine what you went through, though. I don't know what I would do if anything ever happened to Bethany. It was hard enough with what happened to her father." The deep sadness in Ira's voice reminded Marris of his own pain. Marris had never been in love before, but he could never imagine what it would feel like to lose someone he cared so deeply for. It was part of the reason he stayed away from women for the most part. Getting close to someone with what he did for a living did not bode well.

"You say that like I can just flip a switch and make my mind shut off the bad thoughts. I will never forgive myself for not protecting her, and I will fight until my dying day to free our people from fear and captivity. We are not the animals SLICE thinks we are, and even animals shouldn't be treated so harshly," Marris growled.

The road was dark and seemed never-ending. They set up the safe houses in the woods to make escape easier if they were ever raided. It meant long drives down country roads with very few places to stop, which also meant Marris would be driving well into the night.

## Chapter Seven

His eyes stung as the sun began to rise. At some point in the night, Ira had fallen asleep. The silence had Marris's mind swirling with memories. Now he was just tired and ready to get some sleep. He could feel his own powers waning with his exhaustion. Sleep was important for keeping their powers up. With a couple of hours left to drive, Marris couldn't hold out any longer. Pulling to the side of the road, he shut off the engine and grabbed his cowboy hat to put over his face. Maybe after an hour or so he would be able to finish the trip.

Stretching out as best he could, he closed his eyes and began to breathe slowly, letting sleep take him away. The little girl next to him lifted her feet up onto his lap and rolled a bit, trying to get more comfortable as well. He held her ankles so her feet wouldn't fall and drifted into a deep sleep.

*Bang!*

Marris woke to a slam to his truck. He reached out to brace himself as his truck went spinning around in a circle. The sounds of Ira and

Bethany screaming echoed in the cab as Marris tried to pull himself awake.

"What happened?" Ira called out. Bethany began to cry and panic as the truck finally crashed into a tree.

Getting his bearings, Marris looked out of the window and saw a big black SUV in the road, the front fender dented from hitting the truck. The hairs on the back of Marris's neck stood on end, and his heart began to race. "Ira, get down low, as low as you can. Bethany, get down on the floorboard. Neither of you get out of the truck. Do you understand?"

Both of the ladies nodded their head and began to crawl to the floorboard while Marris stepped out of the truck. The air was a bit nippy, but his blood pressure kept him warm as he stuck his hand in his pocket and took hold of a rock he had in there. He often kept stones and other small objects in his pocket just in case. There was never an excuse to be unprepared.

The door to the SUV opened, and a tall man with blond hair stepped out. He tossed the butt of a cigarette to the ground and squished it under his boot as he moved forward. In the dark, his pale features were shaded over, giving him a menacing look, but Marris could smell SLICE all over him, which meant he was trouble. "Well, well, well, look what we have here. Marris Stratford, you are not an easy man to find."

"I don't like people," Marris answered, keeping his distance, but also making sure the truck was in view.

"Well, that goes without saying. Funny, you are the only one who has ever been able to break into one of our places and escape. You even killed one of our best hunters. You should be tortured and slaughtered for that alone," the man explained, moving farther out into the moonlight so Marris could get a better view of his chiseled face. The asshole looked like he could model for Calvin Klein. What the Hell was he doing hunting shifters?

"Figure if you are going to kill me anyway, might as well leave my mark. I would like to have something fancy on my tombstone, like 'Here lies Marris. He killed a bunch of SLICE fuckers and went down in a blaze of glory.' Or something to that effect. Maybe play some Bon Jovi or Guns N'

Roses? What do you think? Would it look nice?" Marris answered, pulling his hat down a bit over his eyes so the hunter wouldn't be able to see what he was thinking.

"Oh, you think we give abominations graves now? How cute of you. No, I will just make sure we all take turns shitting on your corpse once you are dead. Then we'll just burn you. You aren't worth any more of our time than that."

"I'm flattered. It is nice to know you care so much. So who do I have the honor of killing tonight?" Marris asked, the corners of his mouth turning up at the sides.

"You won't be killing me, fucker. No, tonight is the night you go down," the hunter answered doing a motion with his hand. More hunters climbed out of the SUV and began to move in closer. They formed a semicircle around him and began to press in, guns and Tasers in their hands. One thing about SLICE, they always had more firepower than they needed.

Marris took a step back toward the truck, not wanting any of the hunters to get past him and to the women. Taking a deep breath to calm himself, he lifted his hands up. "My bad, I surrender. You are right. There is no way I can take all of you out. Might as well give up and be on our way."

Just as he got his hand to chest height, he shifted the stone into a large sword. Holding it with both hands, he moved in and began to fight, disarming the hunters first before he did anything else. The hunters jumped on him, shooting and trying to tase him, but he was too close to their friends, and they didn't want to risk hitting an ally. It was part of the reason Marris had taken up close combat. It was rare for them to want to attack him with the weapons they had. "Come on, get him! How hard is it to get one fucking shifter? This one can't even turn into an animal!" the blond hunter screamed as Marris struck down one of the men.

Some of the hunters struggled to get a hold of their fallen weapons while others had taken out daggers and shock sticks. Marris sidestepped and swirled, fighting the men with everything he had in him. Ever since being helpless all those years ago, Marris had done all he could to ensure that never happened again. Protecting another little girl was at stake, and he would not fail again. He stabbed his sword through the neck of one of the hunters and turned to take another down, but just as he did so, one of the shock sticks hit him. He froze as electricity erupted through his body, sending him to his knees.

From behind him, he heard a woman's voice scream out his name and then a growl. He bobbed back and forth for a few moments, trying to gain his composure again. A couple of the hunters had started trying to strap him down and hold him hostage as a giant wolf began to tear into them. The wolf was nearly black with several tufts of gray lining it. Beautiful was the only word that came to mind. It fought with vigor, ripping the throats out of the hunters and clawing into them.

"Where the fuck did that come from?" one of the men cried out a moment before the wolf slashed his throat with its claws.

With the hunters distracted, Marris was able to regain some of his composure. The shock had stunned him, but not for long. As he began to rise to his feet, he heard the click of a gun a moment before the barrel pressed into the back of his head. "You aren't going anywhere. First, I'm going to kill that bitch over there, and then I'm taking you and the girl in. Say goodbye to your little girlfriend."

Marris saw red, and with lightning reflexes, he spun and grabbed the gun out of the hunter's hand. He fell back with a thud, and Marris pointed the gun toward him. "Marris, come on! Let's get out of here!" he heard Ira call out to him. He would have words for her later, but right now he had business to take care of. Most of the hunters were on the ground dead or wounded. Marris should go and put a bullet in all of their heads, but that would be a lot of bodies to clean up. He needed to get Ira and Bethany to safety. Shooting the blond hunter in the knee, he then shot the tires out on the Black SUV before racing back to the truck.

"I told you to stay in the truck, Ira!" he yelled as he slid into the seat. Tossing his hat onto the dashboard, he turned the truck on and began to maneuver out of the ditch. The truck was dented, but it still ran just fine.

"You were going to get killed," she answered, panting next to him. Bethany was curled up in her lap crying and panting with fear.

Getting the truck onto the road, Marris began to race back the way they came. He couldn't risk leading the hunters to the safe house. It was obvious they had figured out where he was and what he was doing. "Then let them kill me. That is what I am here for. I am here to die keeping you safe, not sit back and watch you put yourself in danger. If that happens again, you take the fucking truck and you run. Do you understand?"

"I'm not going to leave you behind. I couldn't do that to you or anyone. You were fighting to keep me safe, and I wasn't going to let them kill you for that." Ira had tears in her voice, and Marris wondered if it was her coming down from the high of the fight or if it was memories of watching Bethany's father die. Either way, it made him feel like a dick for yelling at her. Reaching over he took her hand and rubbed his thumb over it in an attempt to make her feel better.

"I know what you mean. I won't ever let anything happen to someone I am with. Not so long as I am alive. It just scared me," Marris whispered, showing her he wasn't angry with her, more afraid something bad would happen to her.

"I didn't mean to scare you," Ira whispered back. "Where are we going? Isn't this the way we came?"

"Yeah, change of plans. I can't risk them finding the safe house. I need to get somewhere I can send a message in to the safe havens and then find somewhere else to take you. I'm going to get us somewhere that has a hotel so we can sleep for the night. I'm exhausted and need to charge up." Marris explained the plan as he punched the gas, trying to put as much distance between him and the hunters as possible. "Your wolf is beautiful, by the way."

"Thank you. Why didn't you shift? I find it easier to fight that way," Ira asked, rocking a bit to finish comforting the child.

"I don't shift. I can shift objects but not my own body. It is a rare gift from what I hear. My sister was the same way. We always thought it strange, but it makes for good parlor tricks," he chuckled a bit, relaxing back.

"Sounds like it would come in handy. Marris, thank you for all of this. You don't even know us. It isn't right for you to risk your life for us." Ira's voice was quiet and soothing as she continued to rock Bethany back to sleep.

"Yes, I do. It is what I signed up to do. I will protect others for the rest of my life. There is no need to thank me. Just keep that little girl safe. That is all I ask." Marris felt that familiar pain in his chest but said nothing. He stared forward into the darkness of the night, hoping he would be able to get them far enough away from SLICE and to a safe place to sleep soon.

# Chapter Eight

He pulled into the parking lot of the hotel, the sound of his tires crunching from the excess of gravel in the driveway. The asphalt was in dire need of fixing, but that meant the place would be cheap. Grabbing a handful of napkins, he quickly changed them into twenty-dollar bills, and then he pulled out one of the many IDs he used. "Stay here, I will get us a room. We should be safe for the night here."

Stepping out of the truck, he headed to the safety window and rang the bell. An older man came to the window and asked what he needed. After filling out some papers, he had the key to one of the rooms. Wanting to add to their safety, he parked his truck between two larger semi trucks in a shaded area. Moving around to the other side of the truck, he helped carry Bethany, handing the key over to Ira so she could open the door for them. Once in the room, he laid Bethany down on the bed farthest from the door and went back to get their bags.

"You can take the shower first. I will sit out here and keep watch. Try to relax and get to feeling a bit better," Marris offered up, sitting down on the other bed. He reached down and began to untie his boots. It had been days since he had been able to sleep in a real bed and get a decent shower. Rest stop bathroom armpit washing was not the same as a real shower.

"Thanks. I won't take too long. I'm sure you would like to get in there too." Ira smiled at him before heading into the bathroom.

Falling back on the bed, he couldn't help but think about how beautiful Ira was. She was his job right now, but it didn't mean he was dead. When he was faced with a beautiful woman, there was a very real part of him that came alive. Closing his eyes, he thought about a life much different than the one he currently lived in. A life where meeting Ira would mean dates and kissing. A life where he could pursue her and not worry her association with him would get her killed. It was a pipe dream, but it put a smile on his face.

"Shower is free. The water pressure was nice too," Ira's soft voice said.

Opening his eyes, he saw her towel drying her black hair. The wetness gave it a bit of a wave, and his fingers ached to slide through those silky strands. "Thanks, keep the door locked. I won't take too long. I just need to get this stench off of me. I'm sure it isn't pleasant being around me right now."

"You don't smell bad. You smell like a man." Ira giggled a bit. The sound of her laughter made Marris stop in his tracks. It had been the first time she had done that, and it pierced him. Just as he began to move past her, she reached up and cupped his cheek. His breath caught, and he gazed down at her. "I don't know what I would do without you. Thank you so much."

Unable to control himself, he leaned down and pressed his lips to hers. She was short which meant he really had to bend, but the electricity that filled him was overwhelming. He kissed her for several moments, enjoying the feeling of her soft lips and the scent of her fresh skin. It was the best thing he had felt in ages, and he longed to make more of it. Finally realizing it would be best to stop this before it really got started, he pulled away and smiled. "I won't be long."

It took all of his willpower for him to break away from her and get into the bathroom, but he knew it was for the best. The last thing he needed was to get involved with someone, especially someone he was supposed to be protecting. Breathing in and out for a few moments, he then stripped and started up the shower. The moment the hot water hit his aching muscles, he moaned in relief. Showers always felt incredible, especially after a fight. Blood from the earlier fight washed away as he leaned against the wall. He could stay in the shower for hours, but he knew he needed to be out in the main room to keep an ear out for anything suspicious.

Just as he reached for the soap, a small olive-colored hand pressed over his. Turning toward the back of the shower, he saw Ira. She was naked and holding a bar of soap and a washcloth. Marris froze, hoping his body wouldn't react the way it really wanted to. "Umm, what are you doing?"

"I thought you could use some help washing your back," Ira whispered, heat filling her words. There was no question why she was in his shower now, and he couldn't fight it. He couldn't remember the last time he was with a woman, and he had paid for her. This woman was the epitome of beauty, even more so as she stood naked before him. Her body had sensual curves but was toned and tight. Her breasts lifted just right, with her nipples hard and begging for his mouth.

"That ... is very sweet of you. I haven't had someone to wash my back in a long time," Marris answered, but he couldn't care less about his back being washed.

Shaking, he stood there and watched her soap up the cloth and move closer to him to wash him. Everything in him wanted to reach out to her, pin her to the wall, and take her with everything he had in him. Softly her hand ran over his body, using the cloth to clean him. It was gentle and soothing and had every nerve in his body on fire. "Your body is so hard, so strong. You are beautiful."

"I have never been called beautiful." He growled like an animal, wanting to show her that he desired her as much as she seemed to want him.

"Well, you are," Ira said, turning her eyes up to him. Her hand had stopped, gripping at his hard cock. The soap was smooth and slick, and the warmth of her hand made him want to thrust against her. No, he wanted more.

Leaning down, he crashed his lips against hers, but this time it wasn't a gentle kiss. This was a kiss of hunger and need. He pulled her into him, feeling the length of her as their tongues danced between them. Gripping her hips, he lifted her up wrapping her legs around him. Slamming her against the wall, he kissed her more frantically. For a moment, he thought she would push him away, but when she didn't, he became even more ravenous than he was before. His kisses moved down her neck, tasting the mix of her skin and the water. Sweet sounds of her pleasure began to fill his ears, making his throbbing flesh harden even more.

The passion had risen to levels of insanity, and he lifted her legs higher. When their lips met again, he thrust himself deep into her. She cried out into his mouth as he began to fuck her hard and wild. She broke away from him, and her head leaned back as she gifted him with beautiful sounds of passion. Dipping his head, he took one of her taut nipples into his mouth, sucking and nibbling as his hips pounded wildly.

"Oh fuck, Marris. Don't stop, please don't stop!" Ira cried out, her nails biting into his shoulder.

"I won't, I swear, I won't. You are so beautiful, so sexy." Marris groaned, kissing her again.

Their bodies rocked together in a frenzy of passion and pleasure. He felt her tightening, and his body was building up to what was sure to be an amazing orgasm. Panting and moaning, he thrust harder and faster, hitting the end of her with force. Every move he made had her pleading with him to make her come, and that was exactly what he planned to do. Gone were any thoughts of doing the right thing, of following his mission. All that mattered now was the woman in his arms. His fingers gripped deep into her perfect ass.

"Marris! I'm going to come! Marris! Marris!" she chanted a moment before her body constricted against him. She writhed in his arms as she reached her climax, and with a few more thrust of his hips, he found himself spilling deep inside of her. His cries of pleasure echoed hers as they locked together, lost to their release.

It took him some time, breathing, and leaning into the wall before he was able to set her down and pull away. He still craved her, wanted to spend all night making love to her, but he knew they couldn't. Bethany was in the other room, and there were teams of hunters out to capture and kill them. There simply wasn't time for them to get lost in each other. "Ira," he whispered, reaching out and stroking her soaking wet hair.

Her green eyes looked up at him with hope and caring. Not love, it was too soon, and they didn't know nearly enough about each other for that, but there was something there. "I know we can't really be together. I'm not asking for anything like that. I just needed to feel like a woman again, and you ..."

"Come on, let me get cleaned up. We don't need to say anything. I know the life we live." Marris felt cold saying those words. He wanted to give her more, but it was an impossibility they would both have to live with.

After washing off, he got out of the shower and dried. Grabbing a couple of the dry towels, he shifted them into clean clothes for him and dressed. All the while, Ira stood there watching

196

him. She smiled at him and said nothing. The sadness in her eyes was the only thing that gave away her feelings. She knew as well as he did that getting close was dangerous.

"We should get some sleep. We will be hitting the road early in the morning. I can't risk them catching up to us," Marris explained.

"Yeah, that sounds like a good plan. I'll lay down with Bethany. Sleep well," Ira answered, slipping out of the bathroom.

"Yeah ... good plan."

# Chapter Nine

Morning came too quickly, and Marris was sore from the crappy bed. At least it was better than sleeping in the truck all the time. He was starting to think he would never have a good bed to sleep in. Not that it mattered.

Sitting on the side of the bed, he looked over to see Ira still wrapped around Bethany. She held the small child like she was the most precious thing in the world, which she was. It made him smile. Reaching over, he lightly tapped at Ira's arm so he could wake her gently. "Ira, wake up. We need to get going."

A soft moan, followed by a shifting of her body, was the only answer he got. Bethany, however, woke up pretty quickly. She sat up, looked around, and then hopped out of the bed to rush to the bathroom. Ira finally found her ability to open her eyes and smiled over at him. It was strange to wake up to a woman smiling at him, even if she was in the bed across from him. "Morning. Sorry it is so early, but we really need to get back on the road."

"No, you are right. Besides, I can sleep in the truck if I'm still tired." She pulled the covers from her and sat up. Stretching, she stood from the bed and went to check on Bethany.

"Mommy, I'm hungry. Can we get breakfast?" Bethany asked from the other room.

"I don't know, baby. Right now we have to get back on the road," Ira answered.

It broke Marris's heart, and he wondered how many times Ira had to make the choice to not get Bethany food so they could stay safe. It had to be a hard decision, and one he would not have her make if he could do anything about it. "We will get breakfast down the road. There is a diner there that makes waffles. I bet if we ask nicely they will even put some chocolate chips in them."

The squeal of delight he heard from the other room was more than enough to make him smile. Standing up, Marris checked out of the window to make sure there were no signs of SLICE waiting for them. He had just finished scanning the parking lot when he was knocked off balance by a tiny body running into him. Bethany had wrapped her arms around him to give him a huge hug. "You are the best. Thank you, Marris."

"It isn't a problem. Can't have you hungry, now can we? We have a long day ahead of us. Besides, you were such a brave girl last night. I am very proud of you," Marris answered and packed up their stuff. It wasn't long before the three of them were making their way across the parking lot to the truck. Rain had started to fall, and the weather had turned a bit cold from it.

"Marris, you don't have to keep doing that. You are just supposed to get us to the safe house." Ira walked around to the other side of the truck, helping Bethany in.

"I do need to do it. It isn't charity, and I'm not trying to make you feel bad. We are all family, and family takes care of each other. One day, I may need you to repay the favor." Marris got behind the wheel and started out of the parking lot. He had seen a couple of towns when they were driving the night before, and he was sure they would be coming up on a city soon.

An hour later, they had pulled over into a diner for breakfast. To her credit, Bethany hadn't said a word about being hungry since leaving the hotel. She was a good kid, but once they got to the diner, all she could talk about was food. She bounced in the seat next to her mother, impatiently waiting for her chocolate chip waffle to arrive. Marris had ordered an omelet, and Ira had gotten eggs and hash browns. All in all, they were going to eat well. Marris would put in for some food to go before they left. It would ensure they had something to eat later in the day while they were driving.

"Hey, Bethany, why don't you go and pick out some songs on the jukebox?" Marris suggested, handing her some money. The girl happily took it and skipped over to where the jukebox stood against a wall. Turning back to Ira, Marris went on. "Ira, I want to talk to you about something. You know how to fight, and you have seen firsthand what SLICE will do to us. Do you think you might want to help join our cause? We could use people to help with the safe houses, people who can fight and guard."

Ira looked up at him like he was crazy. He understood the reason for that look too. If someone had approached him about joining them just after Donna had died, he wouldn't have wanted to hear it. Grief can be a powerful thing and can take much longer to be able to function through. "I don't know that I could do that. Not yet at least. I mean, I have a daughter to take care of. What happens to her if I get captured, or worse, die?"

"We will make it work. We protect each other. I'm not saying go out there and break into SLICE camps or hunt down hunters. All I'm asking you for is help with the safe houses. Stay at one, help run it, and help keep it safe. Nothing too dangerous, but something we are in desperate need of assistance with," Marris added, keeping his voice down. No one would understand what they were talking about, but it also meant they would be curious.

"I don't know. We are supposed to be going to a safe house, and you see how well that has worked out. Bethany needs safety. I need to be able to give that to her. She doesn't deserve to live like this, running for her life like some sort of fugitive." There was anger in Ira's voice, an emotion Marris understood far too well.

"Think it over some. It will take us a few days to get you to a safe place and settled. Maybe by then you will have had time to put some thought into it. We could really use someone like you," Marris added, deciding pressuring her wouldn't get them anywhere.

Pop music began to play, and they looked over to where Bethany was selecting songs from the jukebox. She danced and bounced as she picked different songs for them to listen to. The innocence and joy in the girl was an unreal feeling. She had been through Hell, yet she still was capable of being happy. Marris was sure they could all learn from that. If only being an adult came with the energy and emotions of a child, life would be so much simpler if the sins of man hadn't corrupted them in their adult lives.

The food arrived, and as if it had called her name, Bethany came bounding back to the table. She crawled into her seat, waiting with wide eyes as Ira cut the waffle up and put syrup on it. She was a cute kid, and Marris was glad he had been able to make her so happy with such a small gesture. Digging into his own food, he hadn't realized just how hungry he was until he had started eating. His stomach cramped at the first few bites, but once he got some food in him, it settled.

"So where are we going now?" Ira asked as she started on her breakfast.

"We are heading south. There are some safe houses down there and less SLICE activity. It is also warmer. Maybe getting out of the north will help, at least for a while. Last I knew, SLICE was focused in the Virginia area, so if we can get closer to Alabama, we may have a better shot of getting away from them," Marris explained as he continued to eat his meal.

"Mommy, why do we keep having to move?" Bethany asked innocently.

"Well, there are some bad people who want to do bad things to us. We have to move to a place we are safe from them," Ira explained in the calmest and most comforting voice she could.

"Why?" Bethany asked yet again.

Marris decided to step in and answer. "Because they don't understand us. People are afraid of what is different, and we are different. They don't like that, so they don't want us around."

"That is silly. If they don't understand, they should just ask." Bethany shrugged and put a huge bite of waffle in her mouth. Looking up at Ira, she shrugged and Marris figured they were done. Apparently, Bethany didn't have any more questions.

When they had finished eating, Ira took Bethany to clean up in the bathroom, and Marris paid the check. He had ordered some chicken sandwiches and salads for later. They would be spending the rest of the day on the road. Hopefully they could get to the Heart of Dixie by the end of the day.

# Chapter Ten

"Don't let them get me, Mar-Mar! Please, help me! Why won't you help me?" Donna cried out, reaching toward him with tiny hands. A man stood behind her, pulling her hair back and trying to drag her down into submission.

Marris fought with all he could, but he couldn't seem to break away from the bonds holding him. He struggled and pulled, needing to get to his sister. "Let her go, you bastards! Let her go!"

Slowly the girl that was his sister faded and was replaced by the image of Bethany. The hunter pressed her back against him, pinning her arms to his chest with one arm while arching her neck back. To the side, Ira lay motionless on the floor, a pool of blood forming from below her chest. Rage surged in Marris, but no amount of fighting allowed him to free himself. He was helpless, useless, and it was driving him mad.

"Shut up, little girl. No one is going to save you." The hunter looked up at Marris, and he saw the man who had attacked them on the road. A cigarette dangled from his lips as he smiled at Marris. His fingers gripped into the dagger, pressing it tighter to *the little girl's neck. "You won't win. We are stronger than you and better equipped. Nothing you do will ever be able to take us down. Give up now. Your efforts are futile.*

*Time stood still between them for several heartbeats. Then, without warning, he sliced across Bethany's neck. Blood poured from the gash, and the little girl fell from the hunter's grasp with a thick thud. Jumping toward him, Marris screamed out in hatred and agony.*

"Marris! Marris, wake up!" Marris lunged forward with a start, pushing at the arms that had been pressed to him. A thud sounded and Marris jumped, moving to attack whoever was after him.

It took him a moment to realize he was in the bed of the hotel room they had rented for the night. Ira lay in a heap on the floor, staring up at him wide-eyed with concern. Sweat covered Marris's body, and he could feel it dripping down his back. Gaining his bearings, he reached out and pulled Ira up from the floor. "Oh shit, I'm sorry. I didn't mean to push you off of me like that."

Ira reached up and stroked his face. Her soft skin was warm and comforting, a strange juxtaposition after the fearful dream he had just experienced. Something about her always seemed to sink deep down inside of him. Reaching out for her, he pulled her into his arms and held her tightly. The image of her dead on the floor continued to flash through his mind, making his body shiver. He had to keep her safe, but part of him questioned if that was something he could really accomplish. He was starting to wonder if he would ever be able to keep anyone safe.

"What were you dreaming about?" Ira asked, her nose nuzzling against his chest. He could feel her breathe him in, as if she had needed the comfort just as much as he did.

"The same thing I always dream about, my sister. I can't shake it. I can't get rid of the image of her being killed in front of me, and it haunts me still," Marris answered, squeezing her a little tighter. He hoped holding her close would keep her safe, but he knew better. His arms could only do so much. There was weakness in him, and his faith in himself was running thin.

"I don't think I would be able to do anything about it either, but you have to find a way to move past it. You can't let the past rule your future," Ira whispered, moving in his arms.

Her hip brushed against his groin, making electricity rush through his veins. Even in the state of fear and panic he was in, he craved her.

"You are one to talk. Our lives don't let us move past it. We live each day with a constant reminder of the pain we were and are forced to endure. You can't sit there and tell me to just move past it. My sister is what keeps me fighting," Marris said, loosening his grip on her and reaching up to stroke her face. He loved touching the satin of her skin.

"It isn't the same. All of this just started for me. I fight every day to not let it bring me down. I don't want to see you destroyed by it," Ira answered, a soft moan in her voice.

"Why do you care so much?" Why he was being so defiant, he wasn't sure, but her treating him like this was foreign to him, like he could just pretend the world was different and one day his sister would come back, hurt him and angered him.

"Why don't you care enough? I care about you because you are risking your life for mine. I'd be a pretty big jerk if I didn't care," Ira answered, leaning up and kissing him softly. Her lips against his sent fire through him and took away any ability to think. All he could focus on was how sweet she tasted and how good she smelled. She fought his anger with her tenderness, but it could not calm the raging beast inside of him that desired her above all things.

Twisting her in the bed, he pulled her under the covers with him, making sure the blanket covered them completely. Their kiss grew quickly, deepening into something more passionate than comforting, and his body became sensitive and responsive to her every touch. It was a spell only she could cast on him, and he lost himself in her completely. He glided his hand over her, pressing her body tightly to his as he rolled to lie on top of her. Hunger took control of both of them.

Ravenous, he began to kiss his way down her body. The way she panted and gasped at every move and touch drove him further. In a quick motion, he pulled her pants down to her knees, not even bothering to take them off. He spread her legs before him as much as he could, pushing her knees down to the mattress, so she was spread before him. The darkness under the blanket kept him from being able to see her fully, but he could smell her and taste her, which was even better. Her hips lifted and rocked, begging for his attention, and he was all too happy to give it to her.

Yanking her panties to the side, he growled as he delivered one firm lick to her core. She yelped in surprise for a moment before moaning and relaxing to him. He swept his tongue over that tender spot a couple of times, basking in the taste of her body, and then he sealed his lips to her, sucking her into his mouth. She moaned and gasped, fighting not to make noise and wake her daughter. The way she writhed below him was sensual and sexy, and her scent put his senses in overdrive.

Marris sucked and licked and nibbled with fever. His fingers gripped into her hips, holding her to the bed so he could control their movements. Stabbing his tongue deep inside of her, he moaned deeply, pulling out as much of her arousal as he could. He was a starving man, and she was the elixir of life. Wrapping his arms around her, he held her so tightly to him he could barely breathe as he continued to worship at her womanhood. Her fingers sank deep into his hair, pulling tightly as her breathing became faster and more frantic. Then she arched and cried out, pulling the pillow over her face to muffle the sound as her body exploded for him.

Not wanting to miss out on the sweet sensuality of her convulsing body, he quickly crawled up her while she was lost in her orgasm. Shoving his pants down as he moved, he slammed into her the moment he was lined up with her. The walls of her center squeezed him so tightly he felt like he had to force himself inside of her. She wiggled and kicked, getting her pants the rest of the way off, and then she wrapped her legs around his waist. Their lips crashed together, and Marris began to frantically fuck her, needing to release inside of her more than anything in that moment.

Grabbing one of her legs, he threw it over his shoulder, changing the angle to take her even deeper. He could feel the end of him hitting the end of her, and that seemed to make her shriek in delight with every thrust he delivered to her. Hard and hungry, they fucked like they were overcome with madness, which maybe they were. His heart ached, knowing they shouldn't be doing this but unable to stop himself. He was falling for her and helpless to stop it. Under that blanket, in the darkness, she was all that mattered to him, all he wanted. It was a runaway train destined to crash.

Ira matched him stroke for stroke, lifting her body to meet him with every thrust. Her arms wrapped tight around his biceps with her nails digging into his flesh, telling him just how much he pleased her. Deep inside, he could feel her tightening again and again. She fought making too much noise, but her body told him she was coming for him, over and over. Pride surged through him, but lust took over, and moments later, he slammed deep inside of her. He jerked and writhed as the ultimate pleasure coursed through him. Fuck, this woman was incredible, and for the first time since his sister's death, he didn't want to fight. He wanted to find a way to love her and take care of her. He wanted to find a way to be a normal man with a normal family.

As he collapsed on her, she wrapped her arms and legs around him, holding him closely. The action was so comforting and caring that it brought tears to his eyes, but he wouldn't let them fall. His head nuzzled into her neck, and he gave her several more sweet kisses as he came down from his high.

"We can't keep doing this," Ira whispered, pain evident in her voice.

"I know, but I don't want to stop," Marris answered, kissing her again. The heat under the blanket had built up, and it was hard to breathe.

"We are going to end up getting each other killed if we keep this up." Ira shifted a bit, and Marris rolled so he wasn't crushing her.

"Yeah, we are. We are."

## Chapter Eleven

Over the next several days, the relationship between Ira and Marris changed from working with each other to lovers. Both of them were more than aware at just how dangerous it was for them to act in such a way, but neither of them seemed to have the willpower to stop. During the day they drove. When the monotony of being on the road became too much for Marris, they would stop at a hotel. Most nights Ira would start out lying with Bethany and helping her get to sleep. Once the girl was passed out, Ira would crawl in the bed with Marris. They made love every day, and Marris was sure he was starting to get too used to having her in his life.

They were close to reaching the safe house only a few more hours away. Driving, he kept glancing over to her, knowing he might never get to see her again. Not like they had been at least. Sure, he would stop in when he dropped off new people, but what kind of life would that be. She deserved better than any life he could give her. They should have stopped things long before, but he had been unable to resist her. Now he was sure he would end up breaking her heart.

"Have you given any more thought to joining the cause?" Marris finally asked, needing to break the silence, and his torturous thoughts.

"Marris ..." was all Ira said. He saw her as she looked down to Bethany, the child having fallen asleep from boredom not too long before.

"We could really use you, and you are good. I have seen you firsthand. Please, help us keep this from happening to other people." Marris had never begged like this, but if he could get her involved, maybe he would be able to see her more.

"It isn't that easy. I have Bethany to think about. If anything ever happened to me, who would take care of her? She needs me. I'm sorry." Ira sighed, looking out of the window.

"Bethany would always be taken care of. I would take care of her if nothing else, but Ira, nothing is going to happen to you. I swear I will make sure that doesn't happen," Marris pleaded, his fingers gripping harder to the steering wheel.

"Don't make promises you can't keep, Marris. You can't even promise to keep me safe through the end of the day. We live a dangerous life, and me getting more involved with it only puts Bethany at higher risk. I can't do it. I will stay at the safe house until I can get my life pulled back together, and then I am going to find a way to take care of my little girl. She deserves a better life than this." There were tears in Ira's eyes, but her resolve was unshaken. It broke Marris's heart, but he knew stubbornness when he saw it. There would be no changing her mind. He wished he could keep her safe and be there for her, but she was right.

"I'm not trying to make promises I can't keep. I really will take care of Bethany if I need to. I really do want to keep you safe. I wish I could be that man for you." The frustration was overwhelming.

"But you can't. I knew that from the start. Remember, I came to you. I knew what I was getting into when this started. Please don't make this any harder than it has to be. I care about you, but I know we can't be together. I'm not asking you to be anything more than you have already been for me." Ira explained. She sounded strong and brave, but the truth was, there was still sadness there. They had been fools, and they would pay for it for the rest of their lives.

Needing to change the subject and not think about everything boiling in his head, he went on. "We will be in Auburn soon. There is a safe house just outside of Auburn, and a shifter-friendly diner in Auburn on the strip near the college. Mama Bear's Diner is run by a shifter and her human husband. They have been there for years, and from what I hear, Mama Bear has the biggest heart you will ever find. I haven't had the chance to meet her, but I hear wonderful things. She helps to check on the safe house."

"She sounds wonderful. Thank you for helping me. I really mean it." Ira reached over and squeezed his knee. Marris wanted more, needed more, but he took what he got and appreciated it for what it was.

"The house itself is run by Bruno Chamberlin. He is a nice guy, older. He used to fight the good fight but got hurt. Now he helps run the safe house. He is a nice man. I have met him a couple of times before, and he always has a good story to tell." Marris went on, slowly letting his sadness wash away.

Turning down a small country road, they were only twenty minutes outside of Auburn, but it looked like they were in the middle of nowhere. Unlike the chill of the north from fall coming in, Alabama still had a lot of green and heat. Marris had even turned on the air conditioner in the truck. Not long after turning onto the road, Marris pulled the truck into a long dirt drive that led to a huge house. Though the house wasn't in the best condition, it was big, which allowed for a lot of people to be there. In the back was a small play area. A creek ran not far from it, and trees concealed it for the most part. It was a nice place, comfortable, and well protected. Instead of using public utilities, it had been set up off the grid with solar electricity and well water. Everything about the safe house was self-run.

On the front porch of the huge manor stood a frail old man. He was a bit skinnier than his height would require, and he stood hunched over, gripping a cane for support. His hair had failed him long ago, leaving only a halo of white around his crown, and his face was clean shaven. Dressed in a plaid button up and overalls, he looked like the sort of man you would expect from a southern farm house. Marris sometimes wondered if one day he would find Bruno with a pitch fork in hand.

Marris through the truck in park and smiled over to Ira. "That is Bruno. He is going to take care of you now. Don't let his appearance fool you. He is still a tough guy."

Ira gave him an unsure smile before reaching to open the door. Bethany followed her out, and Marris exited from the other side. Walking up to the porch, he held his hand out to the older man in greeting. "Hey, ol' man! It is good to see you. Been a while."

"Yeah, well, I ain't going anywhere. So, who have you got for me this time? You weren't followed, were you?" Bruno was nice, but cautious, and that fact showed in his voice.

"No, we weren't followed. I had a run-in right after I picked her up, but we lost them somewhere in Virginia. Since then, I haven't seen any trace of those bastards," Marris answered. "This is Ira Connors and her daughter Bethany. Bethany's dad was killed about a month ago, and they are looking for refuge until they can get back on their feet."

"I see, well, you came to the right place. We have a pretty good record here of keeping our people safe, and I mean to uphold that. Right now I have several rooms available. I can get you two right next to each other so you can get some privacy," Bruno said.

Looking at Ira, Marris leaned in and gave her a hug. He breathed in the sweet scent of her skin and the warmth of her body. "I will check in on you as soon as I can. I swear it to you."

Saying nothing, Ira pulled away and took Bethany's hand, walking with Bruno into the house. Marris stayed there, watching until the door was closed and then turned to go back to his truck. He hadn't expected it to bother him so badly. This was all part of his job, and she had a life to live. Getting back into his truck, he needed a drink and to put some time and space between him and the girl he wished would have been able to stay with him. He was less than a mile down the road when he heard a thunderous sound and the ground shook. Looking in his rearview mirror, all he saw was smoke.

# Chapter Twelve

Marris slammed on the brakes, his truck screeching to a halt. Shifting and turning his truck around, he raced back the way he had just come. His heart pounded within the confines of his chest. All he could think about was he had sworn they would be safe. He hadn't been gone for more than ten minutes when he had heard the explosion. Pressing the pedal down, he pushed his truck to the heights of its ability. How could someone have gotten to them so quickly?

Twisting and turning down the road, he hit the dirt drive at such a breakneck speed the truck swerved into a tailspin. Smoke and dust filled the air, making it hard to see as he approached the manor house. Screams of people echoed toward him as he pushed out of the truck and toward where the fire was burning. All he could think about was getting Ira and Bethany. After all this time, how was it he was still being plagued by the sins of his past? Once again, he had failed the people he was sworn to protect.

Reaching to the front porch, he saw a good half of the house was in flames. A bomb of some sort seemed to have gone off. Bruno hobbled out of the front door, coughing from the excess of smoke. "Bruno! What happened? Where is Ira?" Marris called out, reaching the old timer and helping to steady him.

"I don't know. The attack came out of nowhere. There can't be much time. I'm sure they will be here soon." Bruno coughed again, staggering against Marris.

"Shit! Here, get in the back. I will get you out of here. I will get as many of you as I can out of here." Marris leaned Bruno against the back of his truck and raced into the blazing house. Everyone he passed he instructed to get out to his truck. He wouldn't be able to take them all, but he damn sure was going to try.

Taking the stairs two and three at a time, he called out for Ira and Bethany. Neither of them answered him, and the smoke became denser the farther into the house he went. He lifted his shirt over his mouth and nose to help him breathe, but the oxygen grew thin, and he knew he was running out of time. Finally the sounds of a young girl crying stopped him in his tracks. He looked around frantically, spotting Bethany on the ground.

The child clung to her left leg, crying and screaming as she bled. Marris pulled his shirt off and rushed toward her. Tearing strips of fabric off, he fell to his knees and began to work. "Bethany, I'm here. Let me look at it. Let me help you."

Bethany looked up at him, her eyes like glass from all the tears. Her left leg was mutilated, so he made a tourniquet to stop the bleeding as best he could. It would probably have to be amputated, but he was no doctor. "Why? Why? Mommy!" Bethany screamed over and over, in inconsolable hysterics.

Marris looked over and saw what Bethany was screaming at. On the ground, arm stretched out to her daughter, was what remained of Ira. She had been blown nearly in half from the blast. Pain shot through Marris's heart, and he had to fight his own desire to scream out from agony. Now was not the time to feel such anguish. Later, when he got the girl and everyone else to safety, he would be able to mourn. Not now though. Now was the time to act.

Lifting Bethany in his arms, he carried her down the stairs to get her into the truck. All the while she screamed and cried, trying to get back to her mother. Marris felt for the girl. She was an orphan, alone in a world that hated her. It had all happened so fast too. "Bruno! Make room! We got to get out of here!"

The old man looked up and began to bark orders. He tossed some keys to another man who headed for another vehicle. Down the drive, dust was kicking up from approaching SUVs on the move to take out what remained of the shifters there. Most of them were hurt, and the few that weren't were in a state of shock. Only a handful of people actually seemed to be able to react and accomplish helping.

At the truck, Marris laid Bethany down on Bruno's lap. She was still breathing fairly heavily and burns marred several spots on her body. They were scars she would live with for the rest of her life. He just hoped that was longer than the next few minutes. "Bruno, I need you to keep pressure on her. That leg will probably have to be taken, but we need to get her to a doctor first. For now, we got to get out of here."

"I thought you said they didn't follow you!" Bruno yelled but did as he was told. He held the girl and did all he could to take care of her. The bed of Marris's truck was full of people in various conditions both physically and mentally. Marris didn't care. He slammed on the gas and went flying down the drive, cutting through to the woods to get around the SLICE agents.

"Hang on, everyone! It's going to get bumpy!" he called out a little too late. Groans and cries of displeasure echoed up from his truck bed, but Marris didn't have time to think about it. Getting to safety was more important than their comfort.

One of the SUVs veered off and began to follow them through the woods. He had to weave and dash to avoid going headfirst into a tree, but Marris had been here a time or two and had taken the time to learn the woods. He couldn't say the same for the SLICE agents behind him.

"Listen, if you can shift and fly, do so. The truck will go faster without so much weight. You also have a better chance of not getting caught. If you can't, get as low as you can. It's going to take me a minute to get out of this mess," Marris called out his instructions to the passengers as he continued to maneuver through the woods.

The people in the back of his truck scrambled. Some shifted into various breeds of birds, and others lay down to hide as best they could. Marris flung open his glove compartment and pulled out a bag of marbles. He always kept small items on him for things like this. Today, he was glad for it more than usual. Power trickled down over his fingers, and one of the marbles turned into spikes. Opening his window, he tossed the spikes out, hoping to catch the tires of the SUV. If he could slow it down, then he could get away. He repeated his action a couple of times before he switched up, turning the marbles into lead hammers instead. He tossed the hammers out of the window as well, using as much force as he could in hopes of shattering the windshield. One day he would get smart and buy a gun, and then all he would have to do was turn the marbles into bullets. Today was not that day.

"What the fuck are you doing, kid?" Bruno asked.

"Getting us out of here, what the fuck does it look like I am doing? Just keep pressure on the girl. I know someone I can get her to. I just hope we make it there." Marris didn't have time to keep answering questions. A crashing noise sounded, and he looked in his rearview mirror to see the SUV swerve and smash into a tree. Relief filled him, and he focused on getting out of the woods.

The road on the other side of the woods led to the highway. It wouldn't take long for him to hit the interstate and make Atlanta. The last place he knew John to be was Atlanta, and if he could find John, John could save the girl. With his adrenaline driving him forward, he pressed the gas pedal to the floor. Later he would let it all sink in, but in that moment, he had to stay focused. If he lost his composure, he wouldn't be able to help anyone.

# Chapter Thirteen

He reached Atlanta in record time, hitting the downtown streets like a bat out of Hell. Bethany had long passed out and was starting to run a pretty high fever. Marris knew if he didn't do something, she would die. No matter what happened, he had sworn to protect Bethany, and he would die doing so.

Pulling into the parking lot of an old building, Marris threw the car into park and rushed to get Bethany. Bruno had been grumbling the whole way, but more to himself than Marris. They both knew complaining wouldn't help their cause. Loss was part of their lives.

John came walking out of the building, a cigarette hanging from between his lips as he moved toward them. Upon seeing the girl, he dropped the smoke stick and rushed forward, taking her from Marris's arms. "Tell me what happened."

"I'm not really sure. I had dropped her and her mother off at the safe house outside of Auburn. The next thing I knew, there was an explosion. Her mother is dead; several of our people were hurt. Do you think you can help them?" Marris responded, trying to keep his cool. He was starting to come down from the adrenaline high, and with it panic was starting to set in. Reality was hitting him dead in the face.

"Okay, let's get them inside. I have a doctor friend in there. Maybe we can save some of them." The way John said it, Marris worried there would be more loss than he had thought. John was not the type to beat around the bush about things. If something looked grim, he told you.

"Thanks, man, I didn't know where else to go. You were close, and I knew you had connections. I need to get a message to Ashlynn and tell her what happened," Marris stuttered, running his fingers through his hair.

"You need to go get cleaned up and calmed down. Here, this is Rose; she will take you to a room where you can get back to yourself. I will contact Ashlynn, and then you and I can talk. Stop and breathe for a bit." John motioned for a girl to come over to Marris, and then he walked away, barking orders at everyone in the building.

With a deep breath, Marris followed the girl to another room where he could clean up. The girl, Rose, was curvy with bright red hair and freckled skin. She was quiet, but her smile was warm. "Here you go. There is some soap in there already, and I will get you some towels. Do you need clothes as well?"

"Umm, yeah, that would be good. Thank you, Rose." Marris moved into the bathroom and took off his clothes. Turning the water on as hot as it would go, he stepped into the stream. Memories of Ira flashed through his mind. Frustration, anger, and sadness all welled up inside of him to an overwhelming level. He cried out and slammed his fist against the wall. Tears and cries escaped him, and he found himself collapsing to the floor. This wasn't the sort of emotion he would show in front of anyone else, but alone, in the shower, he could. Alone, he could let go of everything he had built up inside of himself.

Shaking and crying, he let the water rain down on him. How could he have let that happen to Ira? What would he do if Bethany died as well? It wasn't as if he had control over what happened, but it didn't stop the pain or memories. He would still spend the rest of his life blaming himself just as he had done with his sister. Maybe it came with fighting the fight, maybe he was just cursed. Either way it was tearing apart his soul.

Getting out of the shower, he saw Rose had left him some towels and clothes on the counter. Forcing a smile, he dressed and went out to check on how things were going. Most of the people from the truck were doing what they could to administer first aid to each other. John was walking around giving advice and directions. Upon seeing Marris, John walked over. "My doctor friend is working on the girl. She can't promise anything. She was pretty messed up."

Biting his lip, Marris tried to keep his composure. John had trained him, taught him about SLICE, and how to fight them, but that didn't mean he would tolerate weakness, and Marris would never show it to him. "I promised her mother I would take care of her."

"And you are taking care of her. You can't promise any more than that. Marris, you know as well as anyone, our lives are nothing but danger. We can't make promises to keep people safe or alive for that matter. It isn't how it works, especially when you are fighting the cause." John kept his voice and demeanor calm, but Marris knew when he was being reprimanded. John had every right to say it, too.

"I know. I shouldn't have gotten involved with her, but it gets lonely living this life. When I was young, all I wanted was to have a family and be a good husband and father. Now I spend all of my time running around the country trying to stay one step ahead of a group of people trying to wipe out everyone around me. I don't get a chance to fall in love or be anything other than a warrior." Saying it made it so much more real.

"We all wanted other things. I did too, but we weren't given those choices. SLICE took that away from all of us. SLICE has made having a life like that impossible. Until we find a way to stop them, this is our lives, and we can't promise anything else to anyone. We can't promise joy, happiness, and white picket fences. All we can promise is to try and protect each other to the best of our abilities." John patted Marris on the back.

"You're right. I know, but sometimes it is hard to deal with. You have to admit, there are days you wish things were different." Marris sighed, pushing back from where he was standing.

"We all wish that, but there is nothing we can do right now." John patted him once more and then went to check on some of the other people. It would be another several hours before he would have any information on Bethany. All he could do was wait, but waiting was the worst part. Turning to see if he could help, he could at least try to take his mind off things for a little while.

He moved to start helping everyone with getting fixed up. Helping others would help him and give him something to focus on other than his pain. He patched a couple of people up and cleaned another few. Time passed quickly, and hours went by before he knew it. Rose came up to him to let him know dinner had been made for everyone. It wasn't going to be much with the extra people, but at least no one would starve.

Marris had just gotten seated when a tall woman walked in. She had her brown hair pulled up into a ponytail and was dressed in scrubs. "Marris Stratford, I'm Dr. Amelia Rhodes. I have been working on the amputation for little Bethany. It took a lot of effort, but I have her mostly stable.

She will be monitored for the rest of the night. If she can make it twenty-four hours, then I'm sure she will live. Her entire left leg had to be taken. I'm pretty sure even when she shifts, she won't be able to reform the leg. We won't know for sure until she is older though."

"Can I go see her?" Marris asked.

"You can, but she isn't awake. I'm going to keep her sedated until we know for sure she is out of the woods. I wish I could give you better news, but this is all I have for you. I will take you to her now." Dr. Rhodes said.

She led him out of the dining room and toward a set of rooms Marris was sure were once offices. Flinging open one of the doors, Marris entered a room where Bethany lay hooked up to medical equipment. A monitor beeped out her heart rate, and oxygen had been placed over her nose. "How did you get all of this stuff?"

"I used to work for a hospital before things got bad. I still have a lot of connections in the medical world who help me out. The rest I get underground, but I do a lot of research to make sure I get the best stuff. I wouldn't hurt any of my patients by exposing them to bad product. I'm in this to help people," Dr. Rhodes explained.

She stood by the door while Marris moved over to the bed. Bethany was covered up by a sheet. Her pale face sill had a flush to it, but for the most part, she looked all right. Pulling up a chair, Marris sat down next to her and took her hand. Tears began to fall without him being able to stop it. Agony raked through him, and he cried out, laying his head down next to her as he gripped to her hand. "I'm so sorry. I wanted to save her. I'm sorry, Bethany. I'm so very sorry."

He felt a hand press to his shoulder, but he didn't move. He was drawn to Bethany's side and would not leave until she was awake and he knew she would be okay. Then he would go and get his vengeance. No matter what, he would make them pay for what they had done.

# Chapter Fourteen

"*You can't blame yourself for this. You had no control over it, Mar-Mar,*" *Donna whispered to him, crawling into his lap. "You are just one man.*"

*The words were that of an adult, but she was still the child she had always been. Marris looked down to see her big, bright eyes smiling up at him. He was confused, but he would take it. Seeing his sister and not watching her die was far better than what he had spent the last several years going through. "When did you get so wise?"*

"*You deserve to move on, Marris. This girl needs you now. What happened to me, what happened to Ira, none of it was your fault. You have to move on. You are strong. Let everyone see that. I love you, brother.*" *Her tiny hand reached up and cupped his cheek, and then she followed it with a kiss to his forehead. It was the best thing he had felt in ages, and Marris wanted to savor it for the rest of his life. However, he knew it was just a dream, and he would wake up to the Hell that was his life.*

"*I love you, baby girl. I miss you with every fiber of my being. I will do right by you. I swear it.*"

*Marris felt himself wanting to cry again, but he pushed back the tears.*

*"You already have. Protect Bethany. Protect our people. I will see you when you come to the next life." With those last words, she was gone, and Marris was alone.*

The sound of the monitor beeping woke him, and Marris lifted his head to look around the room. Nothing seemed out of sorts, and Bethany was still breathing a slow steady breath. Reaching out, he petted her head, wishing he would have better news for her when she woke. This was no life for a little girl, but it was the only one he could give her.

Sitting up straight, he saw Dr. Rhodes leaned up against a wall asleep as well. She had her feet propped up on a counter and her arms crossed over her nonexistent chest. Dr. Rhodes was one of those women who were all arms and legs and no curves. He smiled seeing she had stayed in the room as well. It was good to know she worried as much as he had.

As he pulled himself from the chair, his body ached and popped from the awkward position he had spent all night slumped into. He arched his back, stretching and letting his spine crack back into place. Moans escaped him and he slowly started to come back to himself. Turning, he saw Rose standing there, waiting with a cup of coffee and some biscuits. He hadn't even realized he was hungry until he saw her, and then he remembered he never ate the day before. So much had happened so fast. Walking over to the girl, he gave her a good smile and took the coffee. "Thank you. I appreciate it."

"Not a problem. I'm glad to help. Let me know if there is anything else I can do for you. With so many people here, we don't have a lot of food, so we are making things stretch." Rose smiled and looked to the bed. "Is the girl going to be okay?"

"I hope so. She seems to be doing all right. There weren't any complications over the night, so that has to be a good sign," Marris answered, taking a sip from the coffee.

"We have all been through so much. To see a girl, so young, so small, going through this, it's just heartbreaking. Please, let me know if I can help. I will leave you to your daughter." Rose quickly turned and left before Marris could correct her. Then again, for all intents and purposes, Bethany was his daughter. He had sworn to take care of her, and he would, for the rest of his life. She had no other family, at least not any he knew about.

Heading back to the bed, Marris put the coffee and biscuits on the little table next to him. Dr. Rhodes moaned and started to stir. A moment later she was awake and heading over to check on Bethany. "Her vitals look good. I think she is going to be all right. We won't be able to move her for some time, and I will have to keep a close watch on her, but I don't think we are going to lose her."

"I can't stay here that long. Those hunters have to be taken out for what they did," Marris whispered, relieved at Bethany's condition. Of course, her being alive was only half the battle. She would have to learn a new way to live.

"Vengeance is part of what got you here in the first place Mr. Stratford. Do you really think going after them is going to solve anything?" Dr. Rhodes asked, arching a brow at him.

Marris sat back and took a sip of his coffee. Her question had been a surprising one considering where she was. John had been fighting for the resistance for a lot longer than Marris had. How could she work with him and be against it? "Letting them go won't solve anything either. It just gives them time to come after me and the rest of the people here. If I'm going to keep all of us safe, I have to go to them."

"I realize my opinion isn't the popular one, but fighting them obviously hasn't done any of us any good. Why go after them? It won't bring her mother back. It won't make them stop hunting us. For every one we 'take out,' they train ten more. They use our own attacks against us to get more people on their side."

"Look, I would love to just hang up my boots and not fight anymore. I would love to just take this girl home and give her a good life, but SLICE doesn't give us that option. Not fighting doesn't make them stop. They will fight us no matter what we do. At least if we fight back, they know we aren't going to take their crap lying down," Marris answered. He could see her point of view. It made sense, but it wouldn't solve their problems.

"We all have choices. I made mine, you make yours. I won't tell you how to live your life, but remember. This girl can't take care of herself. She needs someone. What happens to her if you die?" Dr. Rhodes's eyebrow shot up as she stared at him.

"I get it. I don't have a contingency plan. I was her mother's contingency plan, and we all see how well that is working out. I'm just trying to live my life and keep my people safe." Marris knew he wouldn't get anywhere with her. They could argue until the end of time and not get anywhere.

"That is what I am doing too. You do it at the end of a sword; I do it at the end of a needle. We both want the same thing, Mr. Stratford. We just want to go about it in different ways. You should go and get some real food and rest. You need your strength. Bethany will be fine with me for now." The good doctor went back to checking on Bethany, changing her fluids and administering more medication.

Conceding to her, he got up and went to find some real food. The biscuits were nice, but he needed some meat or something more substantial.

Heading down the hall, he used his nose to find the kitchen. Rose was there, cleaning dishes from breakfast. She looked shy and lost in her own little world. "Hey, did I miss all of breakfast?"

The girl jumped and turned with a smile. Blushing, she went and pulled a plate out of the microwave. There were eggs and bacon on the plate, still warm from earlier. "I put this away for you earlier. I figure you have had a hard time of it lately and could use building up your strength."

"I appreciate that. So, what is your story?" Marris asked, lifting the fork so he could start his meal.

"My story is I am here. There isn't much to tell. Before I was somewhere else and now I'm here." The answer was vague and made the hair on the back of Marris's neck stand on end.

"That isn't much of an answer," Marris growled, looking up at her and scrunching his eyebrows together.

"Not everyone is so willing to tell their stories. Not everyone has things they want to tell," Rose answered and went back to washing dishes. Her body was tense, shoulders set. Whatever had brought her to John had not been a happy experience. Normally Marris would press, but he got the feeling it was more complex than he had time to deal with. One scared girl at a time.

Finishing his meal, Marris knew he would need to find a way to look past all of this so he could fight his war. In the end, SLICE would pay for what they had done. Blood for blood, but a nagging voice in the back of his mind had him wondering if he was only feeding them blood not saving his people.

# Chapter Fifteen

*October, 2015*

Marris walked into the front door of Mama Bear's Diner. The last time he had been in Auburn, he had watched people he loved and cared about be blown up. He had pulled his daughter from the fires and driven her to safety. Back then, Bethany wasn't his daughter, but he had made a promise to her mother and had kept it thus far. They were still learning how to be a family and how to help her walk with her new legs, but they were making it all the same.

Now and then, Dr. Rhodes would watch Bethany so Marris could work. She didn't care for his choices in life, but she understood it. They had a mutual agreement to not talk about it. What Marris did for John and Ashlynn was what he did, and Dr. Rhodes patched everyone up at the end of the day. He had told her once she was an enabler, and she had laughed it off much in the way someone did when they knew it was the truth but there was nothing they could do about it.

Now Marris was walking into the diner, looking to help a family who had lost a loved one. Same shit, different day. His work was never ending at this point. The scent of chili and apple pie wafted out to greet him, but the diner itself seemed empty and dark. Walking to the counter, he knocked on the wood, hoping to get someone's attention. From the back, a short slender man walked out. His face was solemn, showing the lines of his age more. "I'm sorry, we are closing the diner early today. We have had a family emergency. Please come back another time."

"I'm not here to order. I'm here to help. Ashlynn sent me." Marris took his cowboy hat off and placed it on the counter next to him. His cowboy image had grown over the years with his leather duster and snakeskin boots. He wasn't sure if it was a phase or he enjoyed the whole Desperado look, but it was his look of choice at the moment.

"I don't understand. We haven't told anyone ..." the man started to say, but Marris lifted his hand to stop him.

"No, you didn't call, but the boy that ran off with your daughter, he had a tail. We followed

SLICE here and found Seth's car just outside of town at a truck stop. I did some research and found out that your daughter was with him. We have reason to believe that when Seth got caught, they took her with them," Marris explained. "Did you ever meet Seth?"

"No, her friend said they met at a pool tournament. We never saw her after that," the man answered, gripping onto the counter.

A woman walked out from the back next. Her face was red and splotchy from crying. She had dark hair pulled back from her face, and her skin was tan like she spent a lot of time in the sun. Under other circumstances, Marris was sure she was beautiful. "You know where Jessie is?"

"Yes, there is a SLICE camp in Oak Ridge, Tennessee. It is the closest one to here, and we are pretty sure that is where they were taken. It is going to take me a little while, but I will get them out of there. I'm the best at it," Marris answered, but it wasn't what the woman wanted to hear.

"Is there anything I can do to help? I mean, she is my baby. If anything happens to her ..."

Mama Bear started to say, but her tears made her voice crack.

"No, just keep doing what you do. I have heard good things about your place here. I can't guarantee you will see Jessie any time soon, but I will make sure you are told what happens. I will do all I can to see her safe." Taking his hat, Marris stood to leave. He could feel Mama Bear's pain.

Getting out to his truck, he pulled out his prepaid cell and dialed Dr. Rhodes. "Hey, Marris, did you find the kid you were looking for?"

"No, not yet. I have to head up to Tennessee. I may be a while. How is pint size?" Marris asked, put the car in gear, and headed toward the interstate. Oak Ridge was only five hours away, six if traffic was bad. He would stop off in Atlanta and see Bethany if he had time, but he couldn't risk something bad happening to Seth or Jessie.

"She is all right. We are trying out a new leg today. It is lighter, so I think she will be able to get around better. I lucked out with this one, I think," Amelia explained. There was a bit of laughter in her voice, and Marris wondered if Bethany was close by.

"That's good. Let me know how she does with it. I won't be in touch the whole time. I'm breaking into—" Marris began.

"Don't tell me. I don't want to know. Marris, one day you are going to go off on one of these missions and not come back. Bethany loves you. She needs you," Amelia scolded.

"Please, I don't have time for this shit. I will be back, and Bethany is going to be fine. She has a whole building of people to help watch over her. Including you and John. I need to take care of this, and I need my head clear." Marris sighed, his foot releasing the gas to slow his speed.

"I know, I know. Look, I'm sorry. I will stop giving you such a hard time about this. I know it isn't going to do any good anyway. Bethany is fine. Do you want to talk to her?" She finally relented, as per their usual.

"Beth, come here, baby. Marris wants to talk to you." There was a squeal of delight that stabbed straight to Marris's heart. It had gotten a bit easier to deal with the memories of his past, but they weren't completely gone.

"Marris! I miss you so much. When are you coming back?" Bethany asked in that high-pitched excited voice kids have.

"I don't know, baby. So I need you to be good for the doctor and old John. They will take care of you. I miss you too, though, kid. How's the new leg? Need me to tweak it when I get there?" Marris answered, unable to stop the smile on his face. He had really grown to love that little girl.

"No, this one was actually made for me. It is pretty comfortable. I like it. Bring me back something when you come home?"

"I will see what I can do. I love you, kid. Be good. I need to get off of here so I can focus on driving." Marris hated making short calls and being gone so much, but it was better than nothing.

"I love you too! Call me soon!" With a couple of kissing noises, Bethany hung up the phone, leaving Marris in silence.

# Chapter Sixteen

Marris had never seen a SLICE facility so heavily guarded. There were more active guards and more cameras than in any other place he had broken into. For weeks now, he had been doing recon on the place, trying to figure out the best way to break in. It hadn't been easy, but he had found where a lot of the guards went to hang out after work. For the last week, he had gone there to drink with them, slowly getting pieces of information from the lackeys. It always amazed him how much people talked when they were happy, drunk, and tired from work.

Having shifted some of his clothes into guard uniforms, and putting a hat on to hide his face, he was ready to infiltrate. Making his way to the front gate, he used his shifted ID badge to get him through the door. As per his usual, he made sure to walk and act in a way that said he was meant to be there. Instead of looking suspicious, most people simply thought he was new. It had been his saving grace more than once.

Heading for the main building, Marris nodded now and then to some of the guards there but never lost sight of where he was headed. The kids inside were young, still teenagers, and needed out of here. SLICE had big plans for the young shifters, and Marris didn't want them to find out what it was.

Seeing the door that led down to the holding cells, Marris felt a familiar rush come over him. No matter how much he said he was doing this to help his people, part of him had grown addicted to the adrenaline. He breathed in deep and then threw open the door.

Carefully, he took the stairs, making sure to keep his head low yet his demeanor confident so he wouldn't tip anyone off. The stairs curved down several stories, and the farther down he went, the thicker the scent of antiseptic, blood, and sweat grew. It was enough to make his stomach turn, but he pushed forward. SLICE wasn't expected to be the most welcoming host, which was just another reason to get these people out of there. He wished he could free everyone, but he knew he wouldn't be able to do that.

Finding a dark hall lined with steel doors, Marris slowly looked around the corner to see who was there. At the end of the hall, a large window was placed into the wall with light shining from it. Cautiously, he walked down the hall, wanting to see what was inside of the room on the other side of the window. His heart pounded in his chest, making him nearly dizzy. He was halfway down the hall when he saw the door to that room open. With a quick jump, he hid behind one of the door archways.

A large black man, dressed in a suit and lab coat, exited the room, followed by a pale, tall woman with long, red hair. They both had serious looks on their faces as if they were unsure of what they would be doing next. Watching closely, Marris wondered what the two of them had been up to.

"I'm pretty sure the female is pregnant. She is showing all of the signs. We need to have a medic go and test her," the large man said as the woman took down notes.

"I will have one sent immediately. What will you do with the male now that he has served his purpose?" the woman asked.

"He can be disposed of once we are sure the female is bred. We will have to be careful she does not become distressed and place the offspring at risk," the man answered before the two of them disappeared down the hallway.

Pregnant? Could they be saying Jessie was pregnant? If he had not been motivated before, he certainly was now. Giving them a few minutes to get out of range, Marris raced to the wall and peered into the window.

Inside the room he saw a tall, slender boy curled around a curvy, dark-haired girl. There was nothing in the room, no bed, no sheets, and no chairs. It was a bare floor, cold and wet from a shower that had been set up in one corner. The kids weren't even dressed, having been stripped of all but a couple of strange bracelets on their wrists. Rage surged into Marris seeing how poorly they had been treated. They were shifters not animals. Not to say Marris would ever treat an animal like that either. It all disturbed and disgusted him.

Seeing the door on the left, he reached for it to see if he could get through. Scanning his ID badge, he managed to get the door open and saw it led into another observation room. Chairs and tables were inside, along with video equipment and cameras. Scrolling through a couple of the files, Marris got a good idea of what they had made the couple do. Hours of the two of them having sex had been recorded. At one point, there had been a bed and other accoutrements in the room, but they had been taken from them. Barely twenty years old, and the two of them had been reduced to someone's sick pornographic desires. Marris was sure the two were a mated pair and SLICE wanted to research what that meant; however, their methods were far from humane, and it made Marris sick to his stomach.

His resolve renewed, he found the door that actually went into the room and slammed through. The two jumped at the sound of him entering, and Seth looked up at him. Marris's eyes grew wide as he saw the boy. He and Seth had met over a year ago in Atlanta, and Marris had found him to be a very enthusiastic and charming kid. What SLICE had done to him was beyond their usual torture. Seth's right eye had been gouged from its socket, leaving nothing but a bloody hole in its wake. There were scars and wounds all over his body, but he stood tall and proud, ready to take more damage and pain to protect his woman.

For a second, it looked like Seth might attack him, but then realization filled his eye. "Marris?"

"Hey, kid, I came to bust you out of here. We need to split quick though," Marris answered, peeking back out into the hallway to see if anyone was coming. Reaching up, he pulled off his jacket and tossed it to Seth.

Seth took the jacket and went to Jessie who was groggily waking on the floor. Her body was shaking as Seth wrapped the fabric around her and tried to help her stand. "Jessie, this is my friend, Marris. I think he has come to help us. We need to run. Do you think you can do that?" Seth turned to Marris. "I don't think we will get far unless you have a good plan. We can't shift. These things on our wrist nullify our magic; besides, Jess is really sick from being pregnant."

"Yeah, kid, I know, I heard. We need to go quick though. I'm sure I can get us out of here if we leave now. I saw two people leave the observation room earlier, and it did not seem like they had good plans for the two of you," Marris answered, holding the door open for the other two. "Maybe we can take someone down along the way and get you some clothes too. You might incite a riot or something running around like that."

That last part got a bit of a smile out of Seth as he moved from the room. Marris decided not to waste time taking someone out. Instead he took hold of one of the chairs from the observation room and shifted it into a pair of pants for Seth. Tossing them to the kid, he gave him a few seconds to get dressed, and then he cleared the hallway. As they moved into the hallway, Seth reached in his pocket and pulled out a couple of stones. He shifted them into knives, handing one to Seth and keeping one for himself. "Jessie, can you fight?"

The girl made a frightened sound, but she quickly recovered. "I'm an Alabama girl. We learn to take care of ourselves at a very young age. I won't hold you back."

Marris chuckled a bit and pushed open the door leading up to the main part of the building. He knew getting them out would be challenging. It always was in the past, but not being able to shift would make it even more difficult. Ideas and plans raced through his mind, trying to think up the best plan for them. Glancing back, he saw them keeping up with him pretty well.

They reached the top of the stairs just as the alarms sounded. "Fuck," Marris whispered, turning to look at the kids. "All right, time to prove it. Don't let them get you, because I can't come back and get you a second time. This is the make it or break it point."

Hunters began to fill the halls, rushing toward where the three of them stood. Seth leaned over Marris's shoulder, his crimson hair falling forward around the both of them. "We just need to make that door down there, right?"

"Yeah, then get past the gates. I have a truck on the other side of the woods from here. If we can get through there without them catching us, we will be good. That's going to be interesting to do without shoes. I might can stop long enough to make you some, but it really depends on how close they stick to us. Hope those Alabama girl feet can handle the woods without protection. Now, let's go!"

Marris heard the two of them inhale and exhale, as if coming to terms with the extreme situation they were all in. This was a suicide mission. Most of the missions Marris took were, but he hadn't expected the kids to be naked and in such bad condition. It was an all-time low for SLICE.

The moment they hit the main floor, guns were fired and people began to attack. The three of them took off at breakneck speeds. *Hit the door, clear the gate, navigate the woods, and off to grandmother's house, or some shit like that*, Marris chanted in his mind, using his knife to take out any hunter who braved getting close to him. He didn't even try to wound and not kill, stabbing into necks instead of arms or legs. Time had turned him into a careless monster when it came to these people, and he exterminated them like the rodents they were.

Behind him, he could hear Seth fighting as well. They kept Jessie in the middle, more because of her condition than her ability, but even she had to fight to make it through the horde of people trying to take them down. Once they reached the door, it would only take a few minutes to get through the yard to the outer fence, if it wasn't overrun with people.

"Two in less than a month, Bridgett, you better do something about this!" Marris heard the angry sound of a man's voice calling from far behind them.

"They are getting brave," a woman responded. Marris didn't look back to see who it was. He didn't care. A couple of weeks ago, Ashlynn had freed someone else. They were getting brave, and they were getting tired of their people being in danger. The time was coming for them to really fight back.

"The gate is just ahead, not far now!" Seth called out. They were close. They were going to make it. Hell, Marris hoped they made it. He had a little girl to get home to.

# Chapter Seventeen

They had just made it to the gate when trucks started moving in with backup. Apparently, SLICE had been prepared for their attack and was doing all they could to take them out. Marris turned to Seth and saw he was wearing thin fast. He had taken too much damage for far too long.

"Marris, you need to promise me something. If I don't make it, you have to get Jessie somewhere safe. Please, make sure she gets out of here," Seth groaned through gritted teeth. He was trying so hard to hide his pain, but it wasn't working.

"No, Seth, you can't do that. I need you," Jessie protested with tears thick in her voice.

"I'm not leaving here without both of you kids, so suck it up and shove that idea up your ass. Now, come on." Marris wasn't about to give up, not after everything he had done.

"We may not have much of an option," Seth groaned, looking over his shoulder.

Marris did all he could to get the gate to open, but nothing worked. The whole facility was on lockdown. It didn't help that Marris couldn't shift into a bird or anything and the kids couldn't shift at all. Frustrated, Marris turned back to Seth. "I can't believe you, Ye O' Little Faith. We are going to get out of here, now stop being a Debbie Downer or I'm going to give Jessie the pants. You are better than that. Now fucking fight for it."

The red-haired woman Marris had seen coming from the observation room was headed their way now, holding a large gun. For such a slender woman, she was quite the Amazon. She held that gun like it weighed nothing, and as she came closer, she flipped it up to her shoulder in a smooth motion. Fucking Hell.

"Hey, we aren't going to get out this way, and I can't climb that fence like this. We got to think of something else, and quick. What about that?" Jessie said, looking around the yard. Marris liked how calm she was through this and was glad his friend had found her. Following her line of sight, he saw her looking at one of the armored trucks. They wouldn't be able to travel in it, but they might be able to burst through the fence with it.

"Now, you are quite a clever girl. Come on!" Marris motioned for them to follow as they sprinted toward the vehicle. All the hunters that had been in it before were now out in the yard chasing them. It was still running though, so all they would need to do was slide in and hit the gas.

Darts and bullets went flying by them as they raced toward the truck. Orders were yelled out from the red-haired woman, but Marris didn't look back. Reaching the truck, he jumped into it, waiting for Seth and Jessie to get there. A moment later, Jessie slid in, but just as Seth went to join them, he was shot. He fell against the side of the truck, gripping for the seat. Jessie screamed and lunged to keep Seth from falling out.

"Drive, just drive!" Seth screamed out, using all of his strength to pull himself into the truck.

Marris didn't hesitate. He slammed the gas and propelled them toward the gate. There was no braking and no stopping, and he couldn't bring himself to look and see how Jessie was doing getting Seth into the truck. More gunshots fired, but his single-minded focus was on getting through the gate. Faster and faster the truck pushed, screaming at the strain on the engine.

"Pull, Seth, pull!" Jessie screamed, crying as she pulled him in.

Just as Marris hit the gate, Seth fell onto the seat over Jessie's lap and the door slammed shut. Wire and fencing went flying, and sparks flew from the charge packs that fueled the electric fence. Marris took the truck down the path, wanting to get a lead on the hunters. They would be after him soon, but it would take them a moment. He hoped to be far enough away they could abandon the truck and not get caught on foot.

"How you doing, kid?" Marris asked, taking a turn a little fast and knocking them all around.

"I'll live, maybe. You still know how to sew up a wound?" Seth answered as Jessie put pressure on the bullet hole.

"Yeah, I'll take care of it as soon as I get us settled somewhere. We can't do it yet, though. You are going to have to not be too much of a pussy for a bit," he joked, trying to lighten the mood. He knew the two of them were too tense from the escape and needed something to take their mind off things.

"Not funny. Just tell me when you need me to get up. Right now, I'm just going to lay here and breathe," Seth answered and groaned.

They hit another big bump and Seth cried out. Marris had wanted to do all he could to keep from hurting his friend, but the road was too rough. Once they were a good bit down the road, he pulled the truck over. "All right, we are going to have to hoof it through the woods here. Sorry, but it is the only way. I'm going to send the truck down the road, but you two start heading up the hill through those trees."

Jessie supported Seth and looked in the direction Marris suggested. Rigging up something to keep the gas pedal pressed, Marris sent the truck off down the road and into a tree. It would throw the agents off a bit while they made their escape. Satisfied with where the truck had landed, he turned to catch up with the other two. With how injured Seth was, they weren't moving very quickly. He was going to have to do something about him, or they weren't going to make it to the truck.

"Hey, let me get a look at that. Jessie, do you think you can work on getting those damn bracelets you are wearing off? I mean, I'm sure they are pretty and all, but they kinda clash with our plans." Marris tossed her a stone, turning it into a pair of bolt cutters.

"I don't understand. Why do these things keep us from shifting but don't have an effect on the shifts you make?" Seth asked, watching Jessie as she began to work on getting the neutralizing band off.

"Probably because they don't have a lot of experience and research on someone like me. I figure they spend a lot of time gathering info on you normal shifters, so they probably had someone work on stuff like that to take your power away. They don't meet all that many people like me, so they have a lot less to work with. Besides, they have never been able to hold on to me," Marris explained while he worked. First, he had to pull the bullet out, and then he had to seal the wound. Seth was a good sport about it at least.

While Marris fixed Seth up, Jessie got the bands off, tossing them as far away from them as possible. She was a smart girl, and Marris was glad to meet her. He only hated how they had met. "You got you a good one, kid."

"Yeah, I know. She is awesome. I just wish I could be better for her. Look at me. I'm not even a full man anymore," Seth sighed, motioning to the scars and burns on his body.

"Why did they do this to you?" Marris asked, nodding mostly to the missing eye.

"I wouldn't give them what they wanted. Best we can figure, Jessie was pregnant from our first time. We fought to keep from making love again, but the more we refused, the more they beat me. When that didn't work, they threatened to take it out on Jessie. Finally they started putting something in our food. They took all of our clothes and furnishing, anything that we could hide or use to calm ourselves down. I have never felt so humiliated in all of my life." Seth watched Jessie carefully as she paced around, keeping eyes and ears open for anyone coming their way.

"I saw some of the stuff on the computer. It looked like they were trying to breed the two of you," Marris admitted, finishing sewing up Seth's wound. He shifted some things around them into other clothing items and shoes for the two of them to make traveling a bit easier.

"They were. They wanted to see what would happen if they raised a shifter from the start. They wanted to learn how our powers worked, and how our spiritual connection to our soul mates work. They are a sick group. Now I have a woman who is lost and confused and will have to turn to a life of running. It fucking sucks," Seth sighed. Marris noticed how Seth never complained for himself. It was always what they did to Jessie and how they hurt her. He was a good man, and Marris was glad he had saved them.

# Chapter Eighteen

By the time they made it to the truck, they were all exhausted, but there was still a long way for them to go. Marris made sure the two of them were comfortable and then headed southeast toward Gatlinburg. He was taking them with him to meet up with Ashlynn. As much as he wanted to go home to his little girl, there was still far too much work to do. Seth and Jessie would need to be taken somewhere safe so she could have her child and the both of them could heal. Besides, Ashlynn needed Marris to help her with something big. Plans were in the making for a real attack.

They weren't far from where they needed to be, only about two hours, but Marris took his time getting there. He took every strange back road and alternate route he could in order to keep from being followed. Stopping just outside of Knoxville, he got all of them some food and rented a hotel room so they could get cleaned up. It was a risk, but it needed to happen. Seth needed to clean his wound to avoid the further complication of infection.

"Hey, I will be just outside. You two need some time to yourselves." Marris smiled, standing outside of the room so Seth and Jessie could have some much overdue privacy.

Pulling out his prepaid phone, Marris was desperate to speak to Bethany. When he was on a mission, he avoided it, but seeing Jessie and Seth together had made Marris miss Bethany's mother more than he wanted to admit. Listening to the sound of the phone ringing, he leaned back against the wall and tried not to hold his breath.

"Hey there, I didn't expect to hear from you so soon," Amelia said when she answered. There was always a sound of laughter in her voice.

"I know, but this one has been a bit hard. The girl was pregnant. They forced the two of them into making that happen, had them locked in a room naked with nothing but each other. It was horrific. The boy really could use your help, but it is too risky to bring them there right now. I'm going to see if I can rendezvous with John and have him take them somewhere," Marris explained, surprised at how much his voice shook as he explained it.

"That sounds awful! Yes, if you can get them to me at some point, I will see what I can do for them. It isn't safe for a pregnant shifter out there. Especially not one who is already on their wanted list." Amelia had her moments when Marris believed she was on his side. Her passive nature always won, but he could almost hear her desire for vengeance when it came to innocent people being hurt.

"Yeah, I will get them there. Is Beth about?" Marris asked, wanting to talk to the little girl more than anything.

"Of course, she waits with bated breath for your every call." Amelia called for the girl, and a moment later Marris was greeted with her sweet voice.

"Marris! I miss you so much! When will you be home?" the girl asked excitedly.

"I don't know, honey. I saved two people and have to find a way to get them safe. Then I have to go help with something else. I know you don't want me to, but I have to be away. I do this so you can hopefully have a better life," Marris said, wishing he could give the girl a better life. It was a promise he had wanted to give her mother.

"You are a superhero, Marris." The naive words of a child, and they pierced his heart down to his soul.

"I wouldn't say that. I just want to do the right thing. I love you, baby girl. I will call as soon as I can, but I had to take a few minutes to talk to you. I had to know you were okay." Memories of her mother flashed through his mind, and he found himself fighting the urge to cry.

"You can call anytime. I love you so much. You are my superhero!" Bethany followed that with a barrage of kissing noises.

They exchanged a few more "I love you's" and "take care of yourselves" before Marris hung up the phone and went back into the hotel room. Jessie and Seth were fast asleep, curled around each other, in one of the beds. Marris was sure it was the first good sleep either of them had had in over a month, and he didn't have the heart to wake them. Taking a seat on the extra bed, he pulled off his boots so he could take a shower.

Once again, memories overtook him. Normally he didn't fret so much over Ira. She wouldn't have wanted that from him, and it made it hard for him to concentrate on his task at hand. Tonight, it was all he could think about. As he showered, he swore he felt her hands on him. He remembered the taste of her skin mixed with the water and how she felt when neither of them could hold back. Letting it go, he let himself cry.

*Mar-Mar, you have to let it go. You are meant for something you don't even know yet.*

Donna's voice floated through his mind, and he fell to the floor of the shower. He sobbed and cried, releasing all the pent-up emotions. All of the people he had tried to save and lost, all of the ones he had let down, finally released into those tears. The weight of things he had no control over lifted, and he felt relaxed. He had done all he could and had done everything in his power to avenge those he couldn't save.

There was a war coming, one SLICE was not going to be prepared for. Until that point, the shifters had run in fear. Ashlynn was tired of running, and so was Marris. They were ready to attack, and slowly they were building an army. Ira would have been part of that had she lived. There would be others, though. It was on the horizon, just in sight. Marris would get Seth and Jessie to safety, and then he would fight. The time for flight had ended. No more would he run. SLICE would be taken down, if it took everything from him.

# Calling the Beast

The snow was so white and crisp, even the moonlight was blinding as it reflected off it. He should have brought his sunglasses. That would have helped, but there had been no time. As soon as he had seen the hunters were coming, he had grabbed his brother's arm, and they went racing out of the back door of the cabin. Running was second nature to them, like breathing and blinking. It had been a part of their lives since they were children, and they realized no one would accept who and what they were. Jax, honestly, would prefer to just kill them all, but his brother, Jericho, had convinced him it would only bring more problems and more people hunting them.

As he raced through the woods, the trees slapped against his long leather coat as he weaved his way through the maze. They had thought they would have some time for safety, to relax and recharge while in the cabin. It was away from everything, but the hunters always found them, no matter where they were. Looking to the side, he watched his brother leap over a log and then spin just in time to avoid slamming into a tree. The agility his brother displayed was second to none and far more impressive than anything Jax could maneuver.

Jericho had a way about him. He was wiry and dexterous, which made it easy for him to dodge things. Tall and slender, Jericho moved with grace. He also had a certain charisma that allowed him to charm people. With his silken voice, he could talk to them and manipulate them to fit the brothers' needs. He had been taking care of the two of them for a long time, covering up Jax's more gruff and inhumane personality. He kept his black hair cut short and spiked, letting his crystal blue eyes shine out from his pale complexion. There was never any doubt Jericho knew how to use his assets.

Jax, on the other hand, was more of a lumbering brute who just ran through things as if they weren't even there. The brothers were twins but very different. Only their coloring gave away the fact they were even brothers. Unlike Jericho, with his smaller frame, Jax' was tall and thick, stacked with muscles. His voice was gravelly, and his dark hair was thick, scratchy, and long. Even his beard was substantial and covered a good portion of his face, making him look more like the animal he held inside of him.

"Brother, we can't just keep running like this. The snow is leaving a trail. We are just wearing ourselves out so they can take us down when they catch up to us," Jericho called out, stopping and leaning against a tree to catch his breath. With not being able to recharge back at the cabin, they both knew their stamina could only hold up for so long.

"We are too weak to use our powers," Jax answered, turning to face him. The night was clear, a perfect diamond-speckled sky, but that did not mean much to them except the hunters could see them better. The edges of flashlight beams could be seen peeking through the trees. They did not have time to wait around and make decisions. If they were going to act, they needed to do so immediately.

"We don't have a choice, brother. This is suicide. If we fly, we have a chance," Jericho panted, turning to see the hunters getting closer. There was no time, and Jax knew it. They would run out of energy before the hunters did, and then they would be easy prey. Shaking his head, he did not like Jericho's plan any better, but it would give them an advantage and help the hunters lose their trail. Glancing one more time toward the lights that were quickly drawing closer, he nodded to his brother. No words had to be exchanged to tell him he agreed.

A fissure of magic filled the air and swept over both of their bodies. They were shifters and as such could take the form of almost any animal, though certain ones were easier than others. Each shifter was different and had the ability to take on different animal forms. There were rumors some could even change human forms or go so far as to change into objects, but Jax was not sure he believed such rumors.

Letting the magic take him, he knew it was going to use up the last of their energy to complete the shift and take flight. Slowly his body shrank, and a covering of light black feathers appeared. Wings sprouted, a beak formed, and his heart started to race. Within a few short moments, he went from his normal hulking form to a large raven. His brother had done the same, and without having to say a word, they flew to the sky. The town was not far away from where they had been in the woods. If they could make it to the town, they might be able to acquire some supplies and rest before the hunters found them once more.

\*\*\*

Lenora sat at the counter, her elbow resting against it and her head in her hand, as she looked out at the snow-covered night. It was beautiful, and she wished above anything else she could go out and play with it instead of being stuck inside watching the cash register. It was no fun to be locked indoors on nights like this, but her mother's dying words still rang in her ear. *Don't draw attention to yourself. Don't use your powers. You have to keep yourself safe.*

She had been too young to really understand those words when she had been a child, but she had always lived up to them. In her life, nothing exciting had ever happened. She made average grades in school, never got involved in extracurricular activities, and worked boring jobs so people would not really pay much attention to her. Nothing was exceptional about her, and she believed without a doubt it was the only way to stay safe, or at least that was what she was supposed to believe. So, running out on her job to go play in the snow did not fit the image she worked so hard to portray.

She sighed as a customer came to her line, and she straightened up to start ringing up his items and place them in a bag. When she had finished with the order, she smiled and thanked him for shopping, trying her best to be pleasant even though the customer wore a scowl and seemed to want to be anywhere but the store. Once he had paid, the man grabbed his bags and left without a word, running into two men who were walking in as he was leaving. Lenora gasped when she saw the men entering the store. She had never seen them around before and figured they could not be local. Even the man jumped back a bit before exiting the store.

The more slender man had a bright yet weak smile on his face. He wore a long leather coat with spiked bracelets and combat boots. There was even a bit of eyeliner under his eyes. His hair was black and spiked on top of his head. The other man was dressed similarly but was very large. He walked a little hunched over and was scruffy and unkempt with long hair and a beard. There seemed to be a sense of danger surrounding him, and it made her shiver. The two of them looked around for a moment and then picked up a shopping basket to move through the store.

As they grew closer to her, the larger man stopped and lifted his nose in the air, much like a dog would when scenting something of interest.

Lenora could feel her hair standing on end as he did that, and then he looked straight at her. For a moment, she could swear she saw something flicker in his eyes. Was it violence? Anger? She wasn't really sure, but she got the distinct impression he did not like her.

Walking toward her, he leaned on the counter. Now with him so close to her, she could really feel the impact of his large size. He looked feral, and it made her shiver even more, "Can I help you?" she asked with a shaky breath. If she had wanted to sound brave, then she had failed miserably. Looking up at the man, her eyes staring into his, made her heart stop as he just looked back at her.

"You need to get out of here," he finally spoke, his thick, scratchy voice sending chills down her spine. It was so rough that at first she had not even heard what he said.

"I can't leave. I still have several hours left on my shift." Lenora had not wanted to come off rude, but she also could not go racing off into the night with a man she did not know. She was pretty sure that fell into the realm of drawing attention to herself, and she wasn't sure that was such a good idea.

"You don't understand. You have to leave. They will get you if you stay here." He spoke to her as if she understood what he was talking about. Whatever it was, he was making no sense to her. At first she thought maybe he was drunk, but there was no scent of liquor on him. Maybe he was crazy. That would make some sort of sense.

The more slender man, who had come in with him, walked over to them with a basket full of stuff. She noticed how alike they looked and wondered if they were related in some way. Leaning in to the larger man, the smaller one whispered, "You can't just order people about. No matter what you think, not everyone knows or understands what we do."

She was sure he had not meant for her to hear him, but she had always had really good hearing. It was something that had bothered her when she was younger. She had not wanted to hear all the horrible things the other children said when they thought she wasn't listening to them. She had just wanted to live her life and not worry about anything, but inevitably she would hear the cruelty of others, and it would chip away a piece of her. After a while, she decided it best to just be alone. She would go to school, go to work, then go home, and spend the rest of the night working on her studies until it was time for it to start all over again.

Both men kept looking at the doors, as if expecting someone to come barging in at any moment. Their actions only made her more nervous. "Is this all you need?" she asked, trying to get them out so she could go back to her normal night. They just ignored her.

"Smell her. She isn't safe here. I won't let her stay here and become a victim," the larger man growled back. His voice reminded her of what she thought a bear would sound like if it could talk. However, his words were rude. She did not smell bad in any way. Why would they want to smell her? The slender man lifted his nose up a bit and inhaled deeply.

"Look, I don't know what the two of you are up to, but this isn't cool. You need to buy your things and get out of here," she finally demanded, having enough of their antics. There was only so much one could take.

Without warning, the two men nodded to each other, then jumped the counter, and grabbed her. As she struggled against them and tried to get away, newspapers and candy went flying, but they were both much too strong and had too firm a grip for her to even try to escape. She screamed out, and other workers in the store came running to help protect her, but there was nothing any of them could do to stop them. The men dragged her out of the store even with people attacking them, hitting them, and pulling at her. It didn't matter. Finally, the larger man just knocked the two people out with a couple of quick punches and then tossed her over his broad shoulder.

"Do you have a car?" he asked, looking at the very sparse parking lot. She answered by biting into his back, hoping it would make him drop her. It didn't. His muscles were like pure steel and obviously did not come with nerve endings.

"I'm not going to answer you, so you might as well let me go!" she screamed, beating on him with all of her might.

"They are coming. We have to get out of here and fast," the lean man said, rushing over to a car and breaking the window with a kick from his foot. Getting inside, he started the car by messing with some wires and then called for the other man to get in as well.

Lenora had thought it would be her opportunity to get the jump on them and get away, but the larger man simply shifted her so he had her pressed against the front of him as he slid them both into the car. He kept her resting in his lap as he quickly shut and locked the door. With his arms holding like a vice grip around her smaller body, she watched him nod to his brother a moment before they sped off into the night. Tears filled her eyes. All her life she had tried so hard to keep from being noticed, and what had it gotten her? Kidnapped.

***

Jax was frustrated. This girl was fighting him at every turn, and though he understood why, it did not keep the irritation at bay. Shaking his head, he finally loosened his grip so she could breathe, and he was promptly rewarded with a slap to the face. Growling, he nearly barked at her before his brother intervened.

"Look, I know this is a bit weird, but you have to understand, we are trying to help you," Jericho said with determination, but the girl was having nothing to do with it.

"Help me! You just kidnapped me, stole a car, and knocked out a bunch of my co-workers. How is that helping me?" she protested, trying to wiggle away. At least she was not going for the door yet. That would not turn out well.

"We know what you are, what you can do. I can smell it on you," Jax continued, holding her to him again so she would not cause any more problems. "There are people after us that want to capture us and you. They would do anything to get us and turn us into lab rats. When I realized what you were ..." He let the words sit there between them so she could feel just how desperate her situation was.

Jericho nodded, and the girl suddenly got really still. Even in the darkness of the car, he could see her features grow pale. She was a beautiful girl with thick brown hair holding just a bit of a wave to it and gray eyes lined with a tinge of gold around the edge. She was a girl with curves and substance but still in good shape.

Everything about her was the type of girl Jax would normally try to mate with. If only she wasn't trying to fight him off so badly.

"How did you know that about me?" she asked, her breath shaky and full of fear.

"We are shifters. We could smell it on you, and I'm pretty sure the people after us would be able to smell it on you too, or whatever it is they do to figure us out. We have been chased for a while now. We had just escaped them in some woods not far from town and were coming in to get some supplies and look for a place to recharge before running again," Jericho explained as he turned onto a more secluded road, trying to keep them off the radar for the time being.

Jax felt her body tense, and he loosened his hold again. "We know all about hiding, but you can't hide from another one of us. It just doesn't work that way. Be afraid, either way, it doesn't matter. If we had left you in that store, you would be dead or even worse come morning."

He watched as a single tear ran down her face, and something in him felt bad for his words. He had not meant to sound like a jerk, but life wasn't easy, and sometimes you had to make the hard choices. This girl had been sheltered from the dangers that came along with being what she was. It was something he was able to tell instantly and knew it would get her killed if she did not learn how to truly protect herself.

"How do I know for sure that you are telling me the truth? How do I know that you aren't the ones trying to hurt me? You haven't even told me your names." There were tears in her voice as she asked her questions, but Jax was not going to give in to them.

"You don't. Plain and simple, but at this point, you don't have a choice either. So you are going to have to find a way to trust us," he explained, rubbing his big hands over her tiny arms, hoping it would make her feel better. "My name is Jax, this is my brother, Jericho. Now, do you know a place we can get some rest? If we don't get rest soon, we are going to be sitting ducks."

For a long moment she did not answer, and Jax started to get really annoyed. He could also sense his brother was ready to ditch the stolen car and find some other way to get them out of harms reach. It would be their safest bet. Taking a few deep breaths, he fought to find a calm center. Losing his temper would not do anything but make things worse for all of them.

"Lenora," she finally whispered and then looked around as if trying to figure out where they had gone. "I don't know where we are. My house is back in town. I don't know where this goes. I'm sorry."

The boys didn't flinch as she answered. At least now she sounded like she wanted to help. Holding her more cautiously, Jax was able to smell the sweetness of her skin. It was like honey and lilacs in the springtime. Never had Jax cared much what a girl smelled like. Girls were not meant for much more than getting out his baser carnal urges. He was never in one place long enough to have a relationship with someone, not that anyone would want to have a relationship with a beast like him. The one time he had tried had ended horribly, so he chose never to try again. Hell, why he was even thinking of such things now was beyond him.

With his mind lost in how soft her skin was and how her hair shone in the moonlight, he did not have time to react when the car suddenly started to spin out of control. Lenora screamed, the tires squealed, and they were sent flying into the snow-filled ditch, causing the car to flip onto its side before coming to a stop. His arms tightened around Lenora. He looked up at his brother who was holding on to the wheel of the car and trying not to fall on top of them.

"Black ice. Are either of you hurt?" Jericho asked as he worked to open the door so they could climb out. His brother might be small, but he was still a very strong man.

"I'm okay," Lenora answered, wiggling in his arms. All Jax seemed to be able to do was grunt his response to his brother as he helped position Lenora so she could be lifted from the car.

Once Jericho was out, he reached in for Lenora. With Jax pushing her up and Jericho pulling, they were able to get her out without hurting her too badly. Then Jax simply busted his way out, not caring if he was scraped up by broken glass or twisted metal from the wreckage. The snow started to fall again, and temperatures were dropping quickly. Taking his jacket off, he draped it over Lenora's shoulders to keep her warm. He would be fine in the snow regardless, but he wasn't sure she was used to such conditions. It was something you learned to live with when forced to be in the wild for most of your life.

Standing on the side of the road for a moment, they looked at the wrecked car. "I don't have the energy to shift and fly. So we are going to have to walk and find shelter. We need energy," Jericho finally said before turning and starting the trek down the icy road. Once again, they were on foot in the snow, making a trail behind them. Hopefully they had gotten far enough away from the hunters that the snowfall would be able to cover their tracks before they caught up to them.

"So who are these people after us?" Lenora asked as they walked down the road, the snow getting thicker and heavier as they moved. The clear night had quickly taken a turn for the worst with a thick winter storm rolling in on them.

"Hunters that work for an organization called SLICE, The Supernatural Laboratories for the Investigation of Chaotic Entities. They are a secret governmental organization designed to hunt down shifters like us. Once they catch us, they turn us into lab rats so they can figure out how we work and how they can use us. They don't see us as humans, so they don't have a particular need to treat us humanely," Jericho explained as he looked behind them.

"So these people just chase after people like, um, us and what? Bag and tag us?" Lenora asked, shrugging the coat higher on her in an attempt to keep the massive thing on her shoulders.

"Pretty much. They got our parents when we were teenagers, and we have been on the run ever since," Jericho answered.

Squinting, Jax saw the edges of a trail a bit farther up the road. Running ahead of them, he looked to see where it led. There were not any tracks on it, at least not that he could see through the snow, but there seemed to be some fence work and other signs of human development. Maybe it would lead to an abandoned house or something they could use to get some rest. Looking back at his brother, he nodded and went down the trail, hoping to find something of use. After going nearly half a mile, he found a small wooden house. There were no people inside, nor did it seem like there had been any in some time.

Breaking into the house, he looked around, finding blankets and a bed, tins of food, and some fresh water bottles that had been stored. It made him wonder if this was a summer getaway home, especially with the small lake now frozen in the back of the house.

Rushing back to his brother and the girl, he motioned for them to follow. Staying the night would allow them an opportunity to regain the energy they so desperately needed and rest up from all of the running, which would help them put more distance between them and the hunters. Rushing back to the house, he found a generator and started it up so he could warm the house up. He checked the taps and found there was running water. He smiled in relief. It was nice knowing they would be able to shower up before sleeping. Checking out the cupboard, he found a variety of canned goods, a bona fide feast in his eyes. Opening the cans, he searched and found a way to heat them up so they could eat once his brother and the girl got there and settled.

When Lenora came in the door, she shrugged off the coat, and Jax found himself staring at her. He had been so concerned with getting her away from the store and the approaching hunters he had not realized just how lovely she was. She was not dressed in the nicest clothes, wearing a pair of formfitting black pants and a collared shirt that was tucked in enough to show off her shapely form. Licking his lips, he tried to get his head back into taking care of himself and his brother. He had no need to get distracted with a woman, but even while cooking, he kept glancing over at her. It was odd, and he was really starting to get annoyed by it.

"I'm going to shower while you finish getting food together. Try not to scare off our new friend here, brother," Jericho teased, heading off to the small bathroom. He was sure the water was not going to be very warm, but with how long they had been on the road, a shower was a much-needed luxury.

Jax had no idea how to handle being alone with the girl. He watched her as she piddled around the open room. She fixed blankets and shifted pillows as if trying to find a way to make things more comfortable. There was still a bit of distrust in her eyes, and he knew if they did not keep a close eye on her, she would run. With their luck, she would run right into the hunters' grasp. She was not experienced, he had picked up on that instantly, and that made her an easy target. Not really sure how she was going to handle all of the chaos they had flung her into, he plated up some of the food and filled glasses of water before he motioned for her to join him at the table.

\*\*\*

Jax seemed nervous, which only heightened the uneasiness she felt while in his presence. She bit her lip as she watched him cook the food and make up their plates. Jericho was in the shower, cursing at the cold water, and she just felt lost and useless. She was not sure what to believe. Never before had she met another shifter, and for them to come to her and steal her away in the name of protecting her only proved to increase the intensity of her fear. Her mother had always told her to keep that part of herself hidden, and now these men had come along and told her they could smell it on her?

It was all very strange to her, but through her confusion, she could not keep her eyes off Jax. His strong arms had irritated her when he was kidnapping her, but when he held her in the car to keep her from getting hurt in the crash, she had felt protected. Maybe she was one of those crazy people who fell in love with her attackers. That would certainly round out her very strange life.

When he set the plate and water on the table, she moved over to him and sat down. He did not say much, but his eyes seemed to be racing with thoughts. She wondered if he realized his eyes told so much about him. Trying to smile, she thought maybe she should start a conversation and see if he would join in or leave her hanging. "My mother told me to never tell anyone that I was a shifter. You really frightened me when you knew what I was."

Jax had been in mid-bite when she spoke, and he looked up at her. "Makes me think your mother knew about SLICE. She should have told you. You would have been safer." Going back to eating, he didn't add to the discussion but let it go. Strong and silent seemed to be his way; frustrating as it was, she could do nothing more than accept it and let it go.

"My mother died when I was young. She probably figured I wouldn't understand," she sighed going back to her eating. "She barely had time to teach me basic shifting, but I managed to learn quite a bit on my own. I wasn't going to let myself be weak just because I didn't have someone to teach me."

He looked at her with something akin to pride, and that stare made warmth spread through her. The fact she had trained herself appealed to him, and for some reason, what he thought of her mattered to her. She went back to eating and looked up every so often so she could watch him. He looked like a beast, and ate like a beast, but she had felt him hold her safe. Deep down, she knew he wasn't just some animal. A crashing noise sounded from the bathroom area followed by a curse before Jericho came out, tying a rope around his waist to hold up a pair of camouflage pants several sizes too large for him.

"Clean clothes are better than dirty ones. I can wear this until I can get my stuff washed up." He even had a bit of a blush on his cheeks as he sat down and looked at his brother. "Way to be a charmer. You look like you are wearing more food than you ate."

Lenora could see Jericho's comment bothered his brother, as Jax sat back and used the sleeve of his shirt to wipe the food away from his mouth. Biting her lip, she tried not to draw any more attention to him. Getting up, Jax went to the sink and threw his dishes into it before heading off to the bathroom. Lenora figured it was his way of saying he was going to clean up as well.

"You didn't have to call him out like that. He wasn't bothering me," she whispered, hoping the beast of a man couldn't hear her whispered words from the other room.

"I have never seen my brother like a woman before, at least not for a long time. He usually keeps to himself. I'm his brother. I have to tease him about it," Jericho answered with a hint of laughter in his voice. "There can be a pull with shifters when we find someone we are compatible with. I think that is why he noticed you so quickly when we came into your store, and why he was so insistent we take you and protect you."

"You two haven't talked that much," Lenora said with a confused look as she pushed away her plate.

"We don't have to talk. Jax and I can say a lot with looks and actions. I can tell you almost anything going on with my brother without him ever saying a word to me. I like to talk and tend to talk a lot, but Jax, well, he has always been the quiet one. He relates more with the creatures inside of him," Jericho answered. Seeing she was done, he took her plate and added her food to his before finishing off his meal. "You take the bed. Jax and I will find places to sleep. We will need to get up early so we can get out of here. If we stay anywhere too long, the hunters will catch up with us."

She didn't know what to say, so instead she simply got up and headed over to the bed. Dusting off the covers, she hoped whoever actually lived here was clean and did not leave their home a mess. The idea of sleeping in some strange person's bed was unnerving, but she was stuck in this situation, at least until she could find a way out of it.

Seeing Jax leave the bathroom, she gasped when she saw that he had trimmed up. His beard was now a bit closer to his face so she could see his features, and his hair was shorter and more maintained. He no longer looked like a wild man and instead looked almost presentable. Seeing her in the bed, he just nodded and went to pull up a place to lie down. She watched him move, his bare chest rolling with muscles as he found blankets and made a pallet on the floor near her.

Like his brother, he was wearing some camouflage pants he had found, but they were tight on him, leaving nothing to the imagination. Hugging the pillow to her chest, she watched him, not paying attention to his brother as he turned out the lights. No, she was happy to watch Jax until her eyelids became heavy and she drifted off to sleep. Maybe she would have pleasant dreams instead of nightmares from this crazy encounter.

\*\*\*

He lay there, tossing and turning. His head was spinning with thoughts of Lenora lying in the bed just above him. She had mumbled and wiggled some, as if she couldn't get comfortable, but had finally fallen asleep. The light cadence of her breathing was enchanting him from his need for sleep. It was distracting, and everything in him wanted to get up and lay in the bed with her, but he refrained from it. When he had gotten out of the shower, she had already been in the bed, looking at him with eyes that were a mix of curiosity and distrust. His mind kept drifting to curiosity. Maybe if they had met in some other way, she would look at him differently.

What the hell was wrong with him?

He was not the type to lose himself to thoughts of a woman. He wasn't even sure he could call himself a man. Not when inside he felt more like an animal. No woman would want anything more to do with the beast other than to satisfy some sort of twisted curiosity. It was best for him to forget the girl, get her to safety, and move on with his life.

*** 

Stretching, Lenora woke up. Only a moment after, the door burst open, and three hunters came running into the cabin. Lenora screamed and Jericho jumped off of the couch. Neither he nor Jericho was prepared for them, having hoped the thick snow would cover their tracks so they could get a good night's sleep. Slowly the hunters filed in and then parted as a woman strutted through their ranks.

She was Bridgett Scarborough, and she was one of the leading hunters and capturers of SLICE. Her thick red hair had been braided and twisted, pulled into a severe bun, and exposed her fair face that looked at them with a mocking expression. Taller than most women and very slender, she was dressed in thick furs and leather to keep her warm while they tracked the shifters. Jax had seen her a few times before, but he was surprised she had been sent after them.

Moving closer to the bed, Jax had an overwhelming need to protect Lenora from the hunters, even more so than his usual need to protect his brother. The agents surrounding them were equipped with stun and tranquilizer guns. He knew he would have to be especially careful to keep from being shot. Jax could hear the panicked sound of Lenora's breathing, and his heart started to race.

"Oh, look boys, the abominations have started collecting more of their kind. I guess they want us to be able to find them more easily." Bridgett's voice was seductive and cunning, holding a hint of pride at being able to find her marks. "We have been trying to get our hands on the two of you for some time now. You are good at getting away and hiding, but apparently tonight you let yourselves find a weakness. You should have sacrificed the girl."

Rage filled Jax as he heard her words. It was times like these that made him happy he wasn't human. For all their talk of humanity, he had never met a human who held an ounce of this so-called definitive human trait. They were all out for themselves. Lenora gasped behind him, and he moved up to his feet, blocking her from the hunters and their guns. A thick growl rose in his throat. He didn't even know what her shifting abilities were or how quickly she could shift. It wasn't like with Jericho. The brothers just knew how to work with each other. Adding her into their escape plan was an unknown he couldn't risk.

"We should be honored SLICE has decided to send the best after us. I would think you would be after Ashlynn Porterfield," Jericho said with a hint of laughter in his voice. Ashlynn was a fairytale in the shifter world. She was said to have the ability to shift into inanimate objects at a rate so quick that she could be lost in a crowd with only the blink of an eye. No one Jax knew had ever met her, and it was believed she was made up to give shifters hope, a goal in life. Jericho was obsessed with her and believed her to be a real person. His brother could be a fool at times.

Sighing, he knew his brother was distracting them. Jax was almost certain of it. If his brother could distract the hunters to focus on him, then Jax could get Lenora out and possibly far enough away to escape. The price, however, would be sacrificing his brother. For the first time ever, Jax was torn. Exchanging looks with Jericho, he knew his brother would be angry if he stayed and fought instead of leaving with Lenora. Reaching back, he motioned for Lenora to move closer to him. He could only hope she would trust him enough to not question his decisions, not when they were in so much danger.

"Oh, Jericho, it is such a shame you are tainted trash. I do love how charming you can be. I might have even taken you up on some of your flirting if it weren't for the fact that you are less than an animal," Bridgett spat out. Even as she insulted him, she kept her voice calm and appealing.

Jericho started to move toward Bridgett, and the hunters all turned toward him. His brother was known for being fast, and they did not want him to get the jump on them. Bridgett stepped forward as well, close enough to touch him. Her face was flirty as she reached out and slid a finely manicured nail down his bare chest.

Oh, his brother was good. Jax would always love Jericho for how manipulative and cunning he could be. Feeling Lenora close to him, he took her hand and squeezed reassuringly. He had no way to tell her his plan or what was going on. Instead, he just had to trust she was witty enough to adapt to what they were doing and quickly.

Carefully moving forward, so not to draw any attention to them, he pulled Lenora from the bed. Her bare feet softly hit the floor behind him. This was going to be bad. The ground outside was covered in snow. There was no way she would be able to run far. Listening as Jericho and Bridgett continued to banter back and forth with each other, Jax continued their cautious movements. This was not a strong point for him. His lumbering body did not like to be soft or quiet in any way. Gritting his teeth, they maneuvered around the bed so they would not trip over it when they raced for the back door to try to make their escape. Jax could only hope there weren't more hunters outside waiting for them to run.

Just when Jax and Lenora got past the end of the bed, all Hell broke loose. Jericho attacked, and the hunters jumped on him. With the hunters distracted, Jax took the opening. He pushed Lenora toward the back of the house so they could go out the back door. Rushing with all they had, Jax kept her body protected from attacks. Lenora swung the door open and cried out as her feet hit the cold snow, but she didn't let it stop her. Pride swelled up inside of him as she kept going even through the pain.

A dart flew past him, landing in the snow, and Jax turned to see four hunters heading toward them. Continuing to block Lenora so she could move into the woods, he faced the men as he eased toward them. The beast within him was clawing to get out. There was no way he was going to let these guys take him or Lenora down. Feeling that familiar magic slide over his skin, this time, instead of becoming smaller, he became larger. Thick coarse hair flowed over his skin, and he fell to all fours. Growling, as his form took on something that looked like the mix of a wolf and a large bear, he finished the transformation with a roar at the hunters. For a moment, they stepped back, stunned and unsure how to handle the large creature now before them. Even Lenora gasped from her position in the woods.

Charging forward, Jax bit into one of the hunters, his massive jaws clenching down into the man's leg. He pulled hard, taking him down as he ripped his knee cap from his leg. Blood splattered everywhere, covering the white snow as the man screamed in agony. This only brought the other men out of their shocked stares and into action.

With guns raised, Jax knew he would have to work fast to keep from getting hit by one of the tranquilizers. None of the men out here seemed to have the stun guns, though, making him thankful for small favors. He could fight through a tranquilizer, sometimes, but a stun gun would immobilize him and land him in captivity. When fighting for freedom, it was good to have an advantage. Shifters had high metabolisms.

Hearing her cry out, Jax turned and realized one of the hunters had gotten to Lenora. She wasn't prepared for this kind of struggle. Even if she could fight, she was barely dressed and surely freezing. Bounding over to her, he bit the man in the butt and slung him over his shoulder. More blood speckled the ground around them, but he turned to evaluate Lenora's condition. He saw the tranquilizer protruding from her shoulder, and his heart sank. She needed to be taken to safety, but there were far too many hunters around them for him to just grab her and run. There was too much risk of the hunters getting the jump on him and sinking a dart or two into him. Turning back to them, he roared out once more, rage like a drug to him.

The couple of men he hadn't already torn into froze. He could taste their fear in the air like candy on the wind. Lenora moaned and gasped, but she couldn't get up and out of the snow. She was going to freeze to death, and that really pissed him off. Rushing the men, he bit into one hunter's arm. The gun he was holding fell to the ground as he cried out in pain from the limb being ripped from his shoulder and tossed away like trash. The other man shot at him, the dart landing instead in his companion a moment before the man fell to the ground in shock and pain. Turning to the one that tried to shoot him, he watched as the man raced away in fear. Good. He had to get to Lenora anyway.

Rushing back to where he had left her, he found her passed out on the frozen ground.

Getting down low, he nuzzled his way under her until he had her on his back. Her body curved around him, but he would not be able to move fast like this, or she would simply slide off. Trotting farther into the woods, he shifted again, holding her tightly in his arms. His heart raced. His brother was probably captured or dead. The sacrifice tore him to shreds, but the idea of losing the woman he cradled to him was even more painful. He wasn't sure how that had happened, but his soul cried out for him to keep her with him always.

All Jax could think of was how his life was forever changed. In just a few short moments, everything had had been turned upside down. How was he supposed to make it without Jericho? It had always been them against the world. Looking down at the woman in his arms, he knew he didn't have a choice. For whatever reason, he was drawn to her, and even if she did not want anything to do with him, he would ensure she was safe from the hunters.

The snow was growing thicker as he traveled deeper into the woods, making him have to struggle to keep going. His body grew colder and colder. He wanted to find a way to get them to safety, but not knowing the area and not being able to shift into anything that could get them away faster, he was left with trudging through the snow.

***

It had taken him hours to find a place they could wait out the vicious storm and the effects of the tranquilizer coursing through her system. A small cave on the side of a hill was the best he could find, but it was better than nothing. Setting her down, he went to search out firewood, hoping to be able to warm them up. It had been a while since he had to make a fire the old-fashioned way, but it wasn't impossible for him. Some things were never forgotten, and he had been trained to survive in the wild.

Twisting the sticks together with speed and ferocity, he was able to finally obtain enough of a spark to set some of the smaller twigs on fire. Blowing and tending, after a solid thirty minutes of work, he had managed to make a good-sized fire for them. Lenora hadn't moved, her breathing shallow, and some areas of her body were starting to turn from being overexposed to the cold. Reaching out for her, he pulled her into his body, next to the fire, and hoped he could get her warm enough to prevent permanent damage.

His mind was racing with worry over his brother and now over the woman in his arms. He had never had to deal with such human emotions before. They tore at him, and he had thoroughly decided he did not like them. They caused pain in his chest and made him feel weak.

Finally, after hours, Lenora started to move. He watched her struggle to find her way back from the daze the tranquilizer had put her in. A soft moan sounded, making his body do things it really shouldn't, and then she blinked those precious gray eyes open for him.

"Hey there, you feeling okay?" He tried to whisper but it came out sounding more like a growl.

It took her several moments to gain her bearings, and then she sat up and looked around. He could see her trying to put together what happened, but he knew she wouldn't be able to. Too much had happened in a short amount of time, and now she was waking up in a place he was sure she had never seen before.

"Where are we?" she finally asked, her words coming out breathy and tired.

"Just a cave I found deep in the woods. I'm sure that if we stay here long, they will find us. We have to get out of here soon, but I figured we would have enough time to let you wake back up." Licking his lips, he hated to rush her, but he knew from experience that staying anywhere too long was not good, especially with the hunters so close. "I won't let my brother's sacrifice be in vain. Do you know how to shift into a bird? Flying is the easiest way to put some distance between us and the hunters." He could see the pain flash through her eyes and knew she felt bad for what had happened to Jericho.

"It all happened so fast," she whispered, seemingly more to herself than anyone else. Looking up at him, she smiled, and he felt all of the air leave his lungs. "Yeah, it was one of the first things I learned to do. My mom said we should always have a way to escape, and not many things can catch you in the air."

Jax smiled at that. A rush of pride took over him, and without thinking, he leaned in and kissed her. For a solid minute he was sure his heart did not beat as the sensation of her lips pressed against his erupted between them. Magic sparked and he knew. He knew this woman was much more than some girl he happened upon. He had been destined to be in that store, to find her. A sudden urge to make more of the kiss took him over, and he had to fight it. There was still a possibility she would not feel the same way about him. Pulling away, he had to catch his breath.

"Jax," she whispered, and it was the sweetest sound he had ever heard. Wanting to kiss her again, he licked his lips and leaned in, but then he heard them. The hunters were far too close for comfort, and if they wanted to see where this would go, they needed to leave.

"This life isn't easy, but you are a part of it. We have to go. We will fly until we can't anymore, and then we will find a way to rest. My ... brother will find us. I'm sure of it." He really had no clue if Jericho was even alive any longer, but he needed the faith and strength hope gave him. Helping Lenora to her feet, he gave her one last kiss and then let the magic take him. He saw her do the same, her bird form lovely, small and white like a dove, as she took flight. Within moments they were in the sky.

He had no idea how they were going to make it, but he knew now he would gladly sacrifice his life to keep Lenora safe. There would always be people hunting them, but now, they would have each other. Staying close to her as they found the rush of air current, they flew off. Perhaps they could find some place warmer. He didn't know, didn't care. So long as he was with her, he knew his life would always be whole.

# In the Heat of Escape

The thick stench of bleach hung heavy in the air. There was nothing like that antiseptic smell to wake up to. Jericho's entire body was aching as he leaned against the hard stone wall. It was dark and warm, making the stink stronger. He would have thought he would have gotten used to the smell by now, but it only seemed to get worse.

For the last three months, The Supernatural Laboratories for the Investigation of Chaotic Entities, SLICE, had been running their experiments on him. It was his own fault, though. He had been the one to sacrifice himself in order to save his brother and the girl. He had known almost instantly that Lenora had been meant for Jax. Never before had Jericho seen Jax react to anyone the way he had her. Forsaking his own life was worth ensuring his brother had his girl.

Shaking his head, Jericho had done a lot of thinking about his brother lately. Since being in this facility, he had not found their parents or anyone else they had lost through the years. Jax was all he had left in the world, and he had to hold on to the fact his brother had escaped and was safe. It was the only thing making the Hell his life had become bearable.

The lock clicked, and slowly light slid across the cement floor. Jericho didn't budge. There was no reason to. Whoever was coming in could drag him off if they wanted him to move. He was no longer wasting any of his energy on them. SLICE had already taken enough from him.

It was her scent that hit him before he could see her. Tall and slender, Bridgett always looked very well put together. Today she had her hair in a French braid like a long, red rope he wanted to yank on, or maybe use to strangle her to death. Yeah, that would be nice. Anger flashed through him, but he did all he could to not camouflage his volitional emotions.

"You stink, Jericho. You really should bathe more," she chuckled, her heels clacking against the floor as she swayed closer to him. When she stepped out of the doorframe, more light flooded into the room, causing him to squint from how bright it was outside of his little cell.

"Then give me a bath. You have seen fit to do everything else to my body. Why not hose me down to appease your offended nose? God knows I wouldn't want to insult any part of you," he answered. His voice was still smooth, something they couldn't strip from him no matter how hard they tried, but he didn't feel like his usual, charismatic self. No, depression and rage had taken root in his soul, taking the light out of his once carefree demeanor.

As if she had expected his response, Bridgett nodded, and two men walked in holding large buckets. Jericho cried out as the men tossed the contents of each bucket onto him. "Fuck! The water heater broken or something, or did you stick the buckets in the freezer just for me?" Jericho panted, trying to hide the fact he was now shaking from his soaked body.

"Well now, you looked like you needed a pick me up, Jericho. Who am I to deny you?" There was laughter in her voice when Bridgett responded, and she folded one of her pale arms over her stomach to help control the laughter that threatened to come bursting from between her lips.

Standing there, dripping onto the floor, he growled at her. It reminded him of something his brother would do. Growling was not really Jericho's way of things. "Right, well, I'm up now. So why are you really here? I'm sure you aren't here just to give me a bath and wash my clothes. Thanks for that by the way."

Calming some, she cocked her hip to the side before turning. Again, the men, who before had the buckets, came into the room placing shackles on his wrists so they could drag him out and down the hallway. Groaning, Jericho stumbled a bit as he was pulled from his cell. Bridgett fell into step beside him, her heels filling the hall with the sound of her dominance over him. "Donovan wants to see you again. Maybe this time you will play more nicely, and he won't have to beat you nearly to death," Bridgett explained as they went up several flights of stairs. The higher they went, the brighter the halls became. The thick aroma of bleach lessened, and the sweet fragrance of flowers took over. Artificial light gave way to natural light, and the warmth of the day started to dry Jericho's dripping clothes.

Spring had sprung, and Jericho had been locked inside for it. When he had been free, and younger, Jericho would always go with his brother, Jax, to find some sort of beach for the changing of the seasons. Somewhere that was always warm during the day and cooler at night. It had been a calming time, and though they had never been able to stay long, it had become a time they valued. It was peaceful and uplifting and gave them extra energy to boost them up after the cold winter. Now that was gone. There would be no beach time for him and his brother this year, thanks to Bridgett and Donovan.

Donovan Wright was the leader of SLICE as far as Jericho could tell. He was a scientist, like many of the people who worked for him, but not hunter—at least not anymore. He had tried his hand at it once, and the brothers had shown him just how lacking he was in the fighting department. Now Donovan dealt more in the politics of things, as well as decided what happened to the beings who had been captured by him. He was the boogie man that thrived in the nightmare most shifters worked hard to avoid. Jericho was not afraid of him. He wanted to kill him, but he would never bow down to some bully who had nothing better to do than play God with beings who had done nothing but left humans alone.

His office was locked away behind a thick wooden door. It was polished and pretty, with ornate carvings running over the deep mahogany, and shone with how the sun beamed in from the windows. Bridgett opened the door and stood to the side. The hunters once again dragged Jericho through the door and tripped him in order to make him fall to his knees. It was as if he was being forced to bow before a king he had not pledged allegiance to. Jericho did not like that, but being chained gave him little choice in the matter.

Thanking Bridgett and the hunter guards who had brought Jericho before him, Donovan stood and made sure the door was closed before he looked down to Jericho, who was still on his knees on the floor. Not being able to really groom himself, Jericho's unruly black hair was falling in his face.

"Well, well, well. Not standing so tall now, are we, Jericho?" Donovan's deep voice resonated with a rich English accent. Jericho could not see much of the man from where he was kneeling on the floor, but he was sure by the highly polished shoes he was wearing, his tall, broad body was covered in a fine suit. Donovan had smooth, ebony skin, which he seemed to take extremely good care of, and his black hair was always nearly shaved from his head, making him look bald. He could have been a handsome man if Jericho could look past his overwhelming desire to slaughter the man.

"I don't have to stand tall to kick your ass. I can do it just fine from right here," he growled. His response was rewarded with a swift back hand across the face. Blood spilled into his mouth, and he felt a couple of his already loose teeth quiver. The beatings were taking a toll on his body, but they had done nothing to his resolve. "Oh, I do love the way you butter me up, Donny. I really wish you would invite me over more often. Maybe we should do dinner."

Donovan didn't find Jericho funny, and he slapped him once more, knocking him fully to the ground. Feeling dizzy, Jericho finally could turn and look up at the man and his massive size towering over him. Gasping for air, Jericho swallowed the blood in his mouth and stared at the man above him, his mind thinking more and more about how badly he wanted to kill him. Donovan was not amused though and walked around his desk to take a seat. "You really should think about helping me more, Jericho. You could be such a valuable asset to SLICE, not to mention you could gain your freedom."

"You have no desire to give me my freedom, and all helping you would do is make me a traitor to my people. I would rather be your plaything until I finally die than betray the people I care about. I have a heart. Something you wouldn't know anything about," Jericho sneered as he found his feet again. Standing before Donovan, he gave him cold dark eyes. How could this man possibly think Jericho would go against his friends and family just to garner his own freedom? He had already made that sacrifice in order to save his brother and Lenora.

"You can think all you like that you are saving your people, if that is what you want to call them, but in the end, you are not helping them at all. We already have a trail on Jax and that girl he has with him. I believe my files say her name is Lenora. We also have a lead on the famed Ashlynn. Once we have her, you will all fall. So, you can find a way to save yourself, or you can watch the genocide of the shifter race. Either way, you will never be able to help your people again," Donovan explained with a hint of laughter. It was a sickening sound that made Jericho want to vomit. "We are really excited to get our hands on your brother's girlfriend. She is pregnant, and we would love to have her child. Think of all we will gain from having a fresh specimen to work on."

Rage burst through Jericho as he crashed into Donovan's desk, trying to get over it to strangle the man. How could anyone who called themselves a human do such cruel things? No, humans were the monsters, not the shifters. "You will not touch them!" Jericho screamed, grabbing Donovan by the collar of his shirt. Jericho could feel his body shaking just thinking of what these sick bastards would do to his family. He had heard nothing in regard to his brother since being locked up, and the fact this was the first he had heard scared him. It meant SLICE was not just using tactics to frighten him. They knew where Jax was, and they knew what was going on with him.

Blinded by his rage, Jericho had not seen Donovan grab the Taser from his desk a moment before. He wasted no time attacking Jericho with it. He wanted to scream, but Donovan threw him to the floor and called the guards to come and toss him back into his cell. Kneeling down next to him, Donovan grinned at his twitching body. "You have time to make your choice. Think on it a little more, but either way, you are not going to win, dog. So get used to seeing me, because this is not the end."

Three men came in, two picking Jericho up, as he continued to shake from being shocked. The other stood guard to make sure Jericho did not gain control of his body and attack them as he had just attacked their leader. With an un-ceremonial toss, they threw him into his cell and slammed the door. Once again, darkness fell over him. They could not capture his brother. No, his brother had to stay safe. Jericho could not give up and would not let these assholes get into his mind. They might do everything within their power to destroy his body, but they would never take his heart.

***

It was a fortress. Ashlynn had never gotten so close to a SLICE headquarters before. It was dangerous, and she was too valuable to them to risk getting caught. Lying on the ground, she looked out at the expanse of the manor house surrounded by large concrete and steel buildings. It looked like a mansion in the middle of a prison, which was exactly what it was. Blowing her thick curly bangs out of her face, she shook her head. Surrounding the facility was a thick chain fence with barbed wire lining the top and middle of the fencing to keep people and animals from being able to climb over it. That was not a problem for her since she could fly over. It was more than likely what she would do, but once she was in there, that would be an issue.

Hearing voices coming close, she pressed down into the ground even more and shifted. The magic rushed over her skin and instantly she looked like a stretch of leaf-covered dirt. In this form, she could still think and hear, but she could not see or move. She was the ground, and she could only experience things as a part of the earth. In all her life, she had never met another shifter who could do this, and she wondered what had made her so special. To her, being the only one to hold these gifts was unfair.

Ashlynn listened as the guards walked past the spot she had been hiding, and then she shifted back to her natural form. An idea hit her, and she grinned. The two guards that had just passed by were not far from her. She could still see their shadows from where she was hidden. Shifting into the form of a snake, she slithered after them. It was rare for her to use a snake form, as she did not like snakes much, but it was a fitting form for her to follow them undetected. When she got behind the guards, she shifted into a large scruffy man who was fitted in a guard's uniform. Lifting her now massive arms into the air, she grabbed both of the men by their heads and smashed them together hoping to use enough force to knock them out. It was something she had seen on television and prayed it would work in reality.

Almost instantly, both of the men fell to the ground, and Ashlynn smiled. Oh, she was good. Turning one of them over, she took in the sight of them and then leaned down to take one of the badges. When she stood back up, she looked like one of the guards she had knocked out. Taking a few moments to slide the sleeping men into the woods and tie them to a tree as best she could with their belts, she then went back to the fence. With the identification badge of the guard, Edward Harper, Ashlynn would be able to get into the facility. Maybe this man had access to the areas she needed to reach.

Finding the gate, she showed Edward's badge and made her way in. She knew the basic layout of the place, having been studying it for several weeks now, but she worried about how it would line up once she was actually inside. It had taken her a while to gather the information, slowly pulling it out of the people that worked there. She could only hope she had enough to get her by. Gradually she made her way through to where the main holding cells were. Rumors were going around that Jericho Masterson had been captured some time ago. Ashlynn had heard a lot about him and his brother, and though they had never met, she knew the brothers were warriors for their cause. There was no way she was going to let him rot in a SLICE facility. Not when he had given himself up to save two others. No, he deserved to be rescued.

She giggled at that thought, the sound coming out more like a gruff cough in her male body. She wondered what Jericho would think of being saved like some damsel in distress. Getting to another locked door, she looked in through the window and saw it was a stairwell that led underground. Sighing, she had a feeling this was where she would need to go to find the man. Lifting the badge, she had no idea what areas Edward had clearance for, but she had to try. The badge beeped and the light turned green. Yes! She was through the door and racing down the stairs. The body she was in did not want to move as quickly as she liked to, making her frustrated, but at least no one was chasing her. Keeping up appearances would be the only way to get Jericho out safe. Besides, if anyone knew who she really was, she would be locked up even tighter than Jericho. There was a prize on her head, one she was not naive enough to play around with.

At the bottom of the stairs, the hall opened up into a line of doors with extremely small windows in them. Two guards were in the hall, and they both looked up at her when she walked in. For several heartbeats, she stood there, in a man's body, trying to gauge if the guards were going to come after her or not. She knew she was out of place, even in the guise of someone that should be there. For all she knew, Edward had never been in this part of the compound.

"What are you doing down here? I thought you were on perimeter patrol until six?" The dark-haired guard at the end of the hall asked, making his way toward her.

Ashlynn would have to think on her feet in order to pull this off. Taking a breath, she shook her head. "Yeah, I know, but they wanted me to come early. They said something about how much better you were at the perimeter, and there have been signs of disturbances on the eastern quadrants," she growled out, acting as if she was a failure for having to be sent inside. She had come in from the west, so if she could get the guards focused on the east, she should be able to get out of there more easily once she had her target.

Now that the guard was closer, she could read his nametag. Peter Cornwall. There was nothing special about Peter. He was an average guy of average height and build with dark hair and dark eyes. Nothing about him stood out, but he seemed confident in his job. When he heard what "Edward" had to say, a smug smirk crossed his lips, and he motioned for the other guard to join him. "Frank stop off at the bathroom on the way in?" Peter asked, clapping Ashlynn on the back with a sense of familiarity.

Ashlynn assumed Frank was the other guard she had knocked out, and she simply nodded in agreement. It must have been something that had happened before. "Yeah, you know Frank. I guess I will catch you later. They wanted you pretty quickly," she answered and watched as Peter and the other guard made their way out of the hall toward the stairs.

Looking at the wall of doors, she knew her next challenge was to figure out which one held Jericho. As much as she wanted to free everyone, she knew there was no way they would all get out of there alive. They would just have to come back for their friends. It was her long-term goal to free all of her people, but she knew it wasn't something she could do alone, and certainly not like this.

Peeking into all of the rooms, she had no idea what Jericho looked like, only that he had black hair and blue eyes. With the darkness of the rooms she was looking into, there was no way she would be able to see such small details. The first two cells, however, held women. Though she had no clue what he looked like, she knew he was a man. There did not appear to be anyone in the third room. Her heart was starting to race. There was no doubt in her mind the facility had cameras, and they would start to wonder why "Edward" was looking into each of the cells. She needed to find him, and she needed to find him quickly.

Coming to the fourth door in the line, she saw a man leaned up against a wall. There was water all over the floor like someone had turned a water hose on and left it there for several moments. Though the room was extremely dark, she could see a hardness to his face, his jaw set tight as if he were clenching his teeth. Anger, there was no other word for the look on his face. Taking a chance, she reached for the door. As expected, it was locked. She lifted Edward's badge to the electronic key lock and hoped it would work. The lock beeped, and she looked down to see the light turn green.

"Oh, I am one lucky girl," she breathed, more to herself than anyone else. Swinging the door open, she looked at the man. "Jericho Masterson?"

The man looked up at her with piercing eyes. She could tell the sudden flood of light in the room bothered him, but he refused to let it show. That already hard face only seemed to tighten more at the sight of "Edward," letting Ashlynn know there was some history here. "Having a sudden bout of amnesia?" the man asked, not moving a muscle. His defiance was oozing from every pore of his body. Oh yeah, he was a fighter for sure, and even if he turned out not to be Jericho Masterson, she would be taking him with her. How could she leave someone like this behind?

Walking over to him, she let him see her eyes, let him see how they changed. For a moment the man acted as if to push Ashlynn away, but when he saw how her eyes shifted, it registered in him. She watched him fight his own desire to give her away. "Yes, I'm Jericho Masterson," he whispered, finally standing up, "and you should not be here. I don't know who you are, but they will catch you, and you don't want to find out what they do to the ones they capture."

"I'm getting you out of here. That is the whole reason I am here," Ashlynn answered, going back to the door to make certain more guards had not been sent their way. The coast was still clear, but for how long, she did not know. Turning back, Jericho was up, and she could see the worry in his eyes.

"It won't be that easy. I have a neutralizer on me. I don't know how they did it, but they found a way to keep us from shifting. I ... I can't just run. They will catch me, again, and then they will catch you too," he whispered. His voice was firm but quiet, as he tried to hide from whoever might be watching.

She loved that he was worried about her, but she hated how these humans had found a way to keep them from being able to shift. It was frightening, because it gave the humans a huge power over them. Jericho held up the shackle on his wrist, and instantly she could feel the energy radiating from it. Moving closer to him, when she reached out to touch it, she felt her body start to lose its shape. She stepped back. If they found out her true identity, there would be no stopping them.

"I will find a way, but I can't leave you here. The longer we wait, the more someone is going to question what is going on. So let's go and figure out how to deal with that when we get you out of here," Ashlynn whispered and went to check the door again. The hall was still empty, which was actually starting to make her curious.

Jericho stepped up behind her, careful to not let the neutralizer get closer to her. Taking a deep breath, Ashlynn stepped out into the hall and Jericho came with her. She could feel his nervousness, and it made her own heart start to race. They reached the door and started to make their way up the stairs. The overwhelming stench hit her hard suddenly, her mind having blocked it out in her rush to find her target. Now that she was moving back toward the fresher air, she was thankful for it. Taking the stairs, sometimes two at a time as they rushed to reach the outer door, she could not help but wonder if maybe this was going a little too easy for them.

Getting to that final door leading to the main hall, Ashlynn looked back to Jericho. He was right behind her, but that worry was still very thick on his face. She knew he doubted they would make it out of the compound. With a deep breath, she pressed down the handle and swung open the door. They had only made it a few steps down the hall when she heard the sound of a gun engaging behind them. "I hope you can run!" she called out to Jericho, and without looking back, she took off toward the rear door. Sirens sounded, and lights began to flash just as a tranquilizer dart went speeding by her head.

This body was too large and awkward for her to run in, and when Ashlynn looked back to see several guards on their tails, she knew she would need to do something about it. Jericho, however, was keeping up well and dodging the attacks from the guns. Giving up on this body, knowing her cover was blown, she shifted into the form of a tall woman with blonde hair pulled back into a ponytail and a lean body capable of moving more dexterously. "Who the fuck are you?" Jericho called out from behind her, but she refused to answer. No, that would just get them into more trouble.

Another group of guards came rushing out of a corridor just ahead of them, and Ashlynn nearly fell trying to stop herself from running straight into them. Taking a deep breath, she knew there were no other options. They were going to have to fight their way out. Looking back one last time at Jericho, she gave him a nod and hoped he understood what it meant. The guards moved in closer and then all Hell broke loose.

She jumped and kicked the first guy in the throat, knowing it would immobilize him and send him out of commission for the rest of the fight. Hearing him gag as he stumbled back, she felt a sense of pride at her actions. Because of the risk of shooting their own people, the guards were forced to switch to a hand-to-hand style of combat, though some continued to use the electroshock wands. Ashlynn took her time trying to analyze each of the people around her before she approached one to attack. Behind her, she could hear Jericho fighting just as fiercely, knowing his freedom depended on the outcome.

\*\*\*

He had no idea who she was, but in that moment, he didn't really care. She had come to save him, a man she had never met, for a reason she had yet to explain. No, he would not let her efforts go without a fight, so he was putting his all into it. His brother had always been the better fighter of the two, but Jericho had his own set of skills. Twisting and turning, he slammed the palm of his hand up into the underside of the guard's nose, shattering the bone in a fatal strike. Without hesitation, he then turned and kicked the next guard after him in the knee, letting the kneecap slip out of place and send the man crashing to the ground. The fighting was a flurry of movement with kicks, punches, and the slicing of knives, and Jericho wasn't holding back. His life depended on it. At one point, he was forced to jump back to avoid a sudden Taser assault he had missed.

The girl with him knew how to stand her ground as well, or at least, he thought she was a girl. She had been a man when they met, but now she was sporting a very feminine body. Not to mention, she moved with grace and fluidity, something really impressive to him. Unlike many girls he had met over the years, this one seemed to know how to take care of herself and would not fall to being some damsel in distress. With speed and agility, she fought of the guards, doing what was necessary to ensure their escape, which was good, because Jericho wasn't feeling particular to the role of knight in shining armor at the moment.

Watching two more go down, he saw an opening and went to make a break for it. They just needed to reach the door. "More are coming! Come on, let's go!" he called out and snatched her hand. The neutralizer he was wearing instantly changed her form. She became shorter and stockier, and her hair was a thick mass of dark curls. Though she was pretty, it was not in a traditional way. Her chest was a little small and her hips a little wide, but it all seemed very fitting. Later he would take the time to really check her out, but running from SLICE was not the time for ogling the chick who had come to rescue him.

Jericho pulled her with him toward the door. They were so close. Guards were spilling into the hall, and he was sure there would be more outside. At least outside they would have room.

Reaching the door, he slammed with all his might, swinging the door back and forcing it to hit the wall behind it. The sun was bright, almost too bright for his sensitive eyes. Blinded, he just ran and hoped for the best.

"Hey, let me lead you," the girl called out.

There was a sense of urgency in her voice. She was afraid. He had been locked inside for so long and had never gotten to see outside of the building, so he relented to her. She had gotten in, so certainly she could get them out. Stepping back some, he let her take the lead, but he could tell the guards were hot on their trail.

"There is a gate just over there. If we are lucky, we can break through and hit the woods!" she called back to him. He had been in the woods when he had gotten caught before, so he had little faith in the safety they would find there.

The gate was growing closer, and his eyes finally adjusted to the sun. The sirens were still blaring causing his heart to race even more than the exertion of his body. Once they hit the gate, they both crashed into it. The electronic-looking mechanism did not seem to want to release no matter how much they pushed on it. It simply would not budge.

"I'll climb. You just get out of here. If they catch me again, it will be fine. They can't get anything else from me. You need to go. Go find my brother and his mate. Tell them I'm okay," Jericho frantically spat out as he started to climb the fence. He knew the barbed wire and possible electric lines were going to be a challenge. He also knew adrenaline could do amazing things, and he had plenty of it coursing through his veins.

"I can't just abandon you. I came to get you. I'm not going to give up," the girl answered, trying to help lift him higher on the fence. He was already making good time climbing over the fence, but the guards were coming fast. Tranquilizer darts were starting to fall just short of where they were at, and he knew they did not have time to wait.

"Fly over the fence! I will meet you! I swear!" He showed her eyes filled with determination and hoped she would listen to him this time. His breath coming heavy and his heart trying to pound out of his chest, he pulled himself higher and higher on the fence.

Getting to the top, he cringed when he found the electric wires. His breath stopped, and for a moment, so did he. Looking on the other side of the fence, he saw the girl waiting for him. He had to make it over. He had to escape and help protect her. After all, she had risked her life for him, a stranger.

With a will he had never known he carried within him, he pulled his body up farther on the fence, fighting the electricity that was now flowing through him. He could feel his pulse in his throat, faster and faster. His heart was going to explode, and then he would be no good to anyone. The barbed wire was coming too. He was going to be a mess by the end of this. More darts flew toward him, but none hit.

"All of you are useless! Shoot them! Get them!" a familiar female voice called back. Bridgett was there, and she was angry. Metal barbs stabbed into his flesh, tearing and ripping at him with every move he made, as he made his way to the other side. The blood flowed over him, dripping down the metal coils.

Blinking down, he could see the girl waiting for him. Twenty feet was a long way to jump, but he had to. They needed to get out of there. With a deep breath, he let go, and a moment later he landed in someone's arms. There was a large man under him, who instantly turned back into the dark-haired girl. Bridgett was almost to the gate, and he was sure she would have no problem getting through. Finding their feet, Jericho and the girl went straight into the forest. Yelling and gunshots sounded from behind them, but neither of them looked back.

"This is fucking crazy! I can't believe we just did that! They are so going to kill us if they catch us again," Jericho gasped, his heart still trying to calm down from the electricity shocking him a moment ago.

The forest was getting thicker, which was good. They would be able to hide better and find their way out. Maybe even find a way to get the neutralizer off him. "I came in this way. Come on, you have to trust me. I know how to get away from them, and it's quick," the girl said, trying to keep her voice down now that they were away from the guards. They could still hear them combing the woods, but they were out of sight for the moment.

Trying to find his breath, he leaned against a tree and pulled his hand up to look at the shackle that was still tight around his wrist. There was a locking mechanism. He had no idea if it was something that could be picked, or if they were going to have to find some hard core power tools to cut it off. Once it was gone, they would be able to make a lot better time with their escape. Walking over to him, the girl took his wrist and examined the shackle. Now that they had a moment to breathe, he could really take a moment to check her out. This was the real her. He wondered if anyone ever got to see this side of her. Licking his lips, he was sure he looked awful, but damn, it had been a long time since he had been around a woman he did not want to kill.

"I can try to pick the lock and get this off, but we really need to get a little further away. Come on, this way." Her soft voice seemed to make his body quiver, and for a moment, he had no idea what she had said. Shaking his head, he began to move with her again. She took him through some parts of the woods that looked untouched by outside travelers. Because of this, he was careful to not disrupt anything, hoping it would keep the hunters off their trail.

Quietly she led them deeper into the thick woods until they came to a wide river. The water flowed fast and hard, and Jericho gave the girl a concerned look when they stood there for a moment.

"They will never cross this river, not on foot at least. Do you trust me?" the girl asked, giving him a wicked look.

He was not sure this would qualify as a good reason to trust someone. They could very well be killed trying to cross this river. "Umm, I want to, but first, there is no way we would live crossing that river, and second, I don't even know your name." He kept his eyes to the river and the raging waters. Yeah, they would surely die if they tried to cross it.

"Ashlynn Porterfield," she answered with a smile. That was when he looked at her. His jaw dropped, and his eyes went wide. Was it possible? No, she could not be her. Licking his lips again, he had no idea what to say. "Look, if we get into the thick of the water, there are no harsh rocks. We go under and let the water take us. We will go down a really small fall and land in a pool. Trust me. I did it just the other day to see where it would take me. There is a cave on the other side of the pool we can hang out in until we can get that thing off of you. I have some supplies there, and I haven't seen any of SLICE's people out that way. I don't think they like the river."

It was a risk, a big risk, but he would rather die in a river running away with Ashlynn than be stuck in that lab being poked and prodded at for the twisted ideals of a zealot. Shaking his head, he struggled with the insanity of their plan, but there were no other options. Moving closer to her, he reached up and brushed some of the hair from her face. They were both sweaty and dirty, and he could feel his blood trickling down his stomach from the barbed wire. If he was going to play with fate today, then he was going to go all out. Leaning in, he did something he had not done in ages. He kissed her.

For several moments, he just let the feel of her lips pressed to his take him away from everything that had happened over the last several months and into a world that was warm and peaceful. Her small hands lifted up to his shoulders, and he couldn't help but think she would push him away. She didn't though. No, she held him close and deepened the kiss. Heat washed over him, and he knew then and there he would always trust her. No, he would die for her.

*\*\*\**

She had never been kissed before, not like this at least. Sure, she had brushed her lips against other men's when she was working and trying to uncover information, but she had never kissed like this. Heat built up in her body until she was sure she would explode from it. Her arms wrapped around him, and she pressed as tightly to him as she possibly could, letting his lips take her to another world.

The blood soaking through his shirt brought her back. Pulling away, she looked down and saw where her clothing was now stained with the crimson fluid. "We need to get out of here and get you patched up," she whispered, surprised by how shaky her words were.

Jericho looked down and then back to the river. Ashlynn could feel his heart racing and knew he was afraid, but he managed to keep the fear from showing in his eyes. "Show me what to do," he said, and Ashlynn smiled, taking his hand and leading him into the water.

It was hard to work their way into the rushing current. The river did not want to show any mercy, but finally they were in the deepest section, and she simply fell back. She felt the water rush over her as she slid away in the rapids, keeping her arms above her head just in case. She hoped Jericho was following behind her, but she was too far into the waves to be able to look. What they were doing was dangerous, but it was still better than staying in a SLICE camp.

For several moments, they were tossed around, and then the waters calmed. Just when Ashlynn thought she was going to drown, she surfaced and looked around. Jericho was near her, standing waist deep in the pool of water. Soaking wet, his long, black hair fell away from his face, and for the first time she got a good look at those striking blue eyes. Her heart fluttered, and she wondered if this was what people meant when they talked about love at first sight.

She had always had a healthy appreciation for him, having heard about him and his brother over the years and all they did to help their people. Now she had more. He was not just a good guy, he was a handsome one. Biting her lip, she walked over to him and pointed to where the hidden cave sat. There was a wall of moss and vines that hid it from immediate view, which would give them better protection while they figured out how to get the neutralizer off Jericho's wrist and maybe even manage a couple of hours of rest.

He nodded and smiled at her. Leaning down, he kissed her again, and her head spun from how hungry it made her feel. This hunger was unlike anything she had ever felt before. It was raw and deep, and she was well aware that food would never quench it. Maybe it was all the adrenaline? Yeah, that could be part of it. Wading through the water, Jericho refused to let go of her hand. He kept her close to his side, and when they reached the cave, he lifted her up into it. She was convinced he was some sort of Superman for him to be able to lift her and help her so much, even with the electroshock and blood loss.

Inside, the cave was dark and damp, and Ashlynn scrambled around to find the small light she had stashed. Getting it lit, she then got out her first aid kit. "Take off your shirt and let me see the damage." She had not meant to sound like she was ordering him about, but she wanted to make sure he was going to be all right. He never hesitated.

Tearing off his shirt, he tossed it aside, and Ashlynn was assaulted by the mass of cuts, scars, and deep bruises that marred a body that could have been perfect. He was toned and lean, a strong man for sure. What had they done to him?

"Do you have something I can try to work this neutralizer off with?" he asked, holding up his wrist.

Reaching into a bag, she pulled out a lock pick kit and tossed it over to him as she went about cleaning his wounds. There was nothing she worried would cause them to have to wait for him to heal. It was mostly surface wounds and bruises. His ability to move was too graceful for him to have any seriously broken bones or severe blood loss.

"What did—" she started to ask, and he cut her off with a nod of his head.

"Not now. I want to sit here for a bit and enjoy the fact that I am no longer there, not dwell on what happened while I was," he said, his voice soft as he worked the picks into the locking mechanism.

She could respect that, so she went back to cleaning and dressing his wounds. For what seemed like hours, they sat in companionable silence. He worked the lock; she cleaned his wounds. There was nothing more to really say, she figured, and she had never been very social. Her whole life had revolved around running from everyone that came after her, so making friends never seemed to be a priority.

A clicking noise sounded, and a spring engaged. The cuff fell to the floor of the cave, and Ashlynn felt his power wash over him. He did not change his form; rather it was more he simply let it flow so he could feel it. She gasped at how it felt to be so close to him with his power riding over his skin. It made the tiny hairs on the back of her neck stand on end, and a shiver ran down her spine. With the cuff open, it was no longer emanating whatever it was that kept their power at bay.

His eyes suddenly looked up to hers, and her breath caught. There was raw hunger in those blue pools, the likes of which she had never seen before. It was not the eyes of a normal man. No man could duplicate what she saw. No, these eyes held an animal-like quality that sparked with electricity.

A moment later, he had her pulled against him. Her legs wrapped around his waist as their lips crashed together again. His hands and arms held her firm against him as they kissed, a soft sound resonating from her throat. He seemed to like that sound because he rewarded it with a thick growl of his own. Rolling them, he pressed her down onto the floor of the cave. His rock-hard body was radiating heat, quickly filling the cave to the point she could barely breathe. Her breath came quicker, thicker, and she was sure she would pass out at any moment.

Jericho moved his lips down the curve of her neck, kissing and nibbling as he went. She shivered and writhed, not used to this spark of sensation that exploded over her skin with every touch he made. More of those strange, soft sounds rose from her, and she felt her hips start to roll tighter against him. It was like her body had a mind of its own and was demanding she do those things. Her movements made him groan deeply, and she thought she had done something to hurt him.

"I don't want to take advantage of you, but I fee—" Jericho ended with another moan and kissed her firmly again.

His words cut through her, making her nearly want to cry. Never had she had such desire, and she could feel it throbbing through every fiber of her being. She had been told before that when a shifter found the one meant for them, it was almost impossible for them to stay away from each other. That was how she felt in Jericho's presence, and she couldn't stop herself from pulling him tighter to her.

"You aren't taking advantage of me. I just, I don't have a lot of experience," she whispered, trying to not ruin the mood. He pulled away and looked down at her with a worried expression on his face. Gently his hand moved to cup her cheek. She could feel his body in a way that left nothing to the imagination, but his eyes and his hand were gentle and made her heart almost ache. Once again, he leaned in to kiss her, but this kiss was softer, more passionate. Their lips glided slowly against one another's as he rocked his hips against hers. The sensation it induced ran through every nerve inside of her, making her writhe even more.

"Then I will be careful," he said, his words barely more than a whisper.

His hands slowly slid up her shirt, pushing it away. Their bodies were burning, and he pressed tighter into her as he kissed his way down her neck and over her breasts. The way his tongue tickled her nipple made her wiggle, and she arched back giving him more access to her body. She was afraid and excited all at the same time, and she could feel that same rush she typically got when she was on the run. Only this time she was enjoying it more. They moved together, his mouth practically worshiping her body as he worked his way down.

Magic rolled over them, and she grinned when she realized he had used his powers to shift them both. Only two that were truly connected could do that. It was a simple shift that removed their clothing, but much more complicated to do to a partner. Here, in her true form, she found herself blushing as he looked at her naked body. She had never been exposed like this before nor had she ever seen a man in all his glory.

He gazed upon her as if she was the most precious thing in the world, and then he slid his hand up her thigh and between her legs. His fingers played over her soft curls before one slipped between her folds and touched the sensitive flesh hidden inside. He rubbed that sweet spot with a gentle twirl of his finger, and she felt a tension build in her body as moisture flowed from her.

"You feel like Heaven," he whispered, moving to lean over her again so he could kiss her. His finger worked faster and harder until she became dizzy and frantic. Her breathing became wild and that coil in her belly tightened more and more. Before she knew what was happening, her body exploded, and she swore she saw stars as she arched back and screamed out his name. Whatever had happened had been the most amazing thing she had ever experienced, but Jericho did not stop. He was far from through with her.

"I don't want to hurt you, so you have to tell me if I do something that does," he told her. She would have laughed if she had been able to. There was no way she would be able to tell him anything.

First one, then a second, finger pushed inside of her, and she jumped at the feeling of her body being invaded. She did not want him to think she had no idea what was going on, even though that was the truth of the matter. As promised, he was very careful with her. His movements were soft as he seemed to prepare her body for him. She had seen him, and was not really sure how that was supposed to work. He was far more blessed than she was sure her body could support.

Again that coil started to tighten, and their kisses grew more frantic. She wrapped around him as best she could, her nails sinking into his flesh as she sought to hold onto him. He pumped his fingers with more intensity, making her body tighten to the edge of its limits, and when she thought she was going to explode again, he pulled his fingers away and replaced them with his hardened length. He growled out as he sank deep into her. A gasp and hiss left her as he shattered the proof of her innocence deep inside.

"Ashlynn?" he whispered with a question in his voice. Shaking her head, she lifted her body to him and encouraged him to continue. She had no desire to talk about her virginity. He seemed to understand her nonverbal response as his hips rocked against hers, his body sliding within her depths.

He wrapped his arms around her to keep the cave floor from scraping up her back as they continued their lover's dance. Never had she thought she would give herself so quickly to anyone, but something just felt right with Jericho. His mouth claimed hers again, and she shivered at the sounds he made as he thrust more passionately. His whole body was shaking as his pace increased, and that already tight coil she had deep inside wound to the brink of her sanity.

Throwing her head back, she could feel herself getting to that point again. The sweet explosion he had denied her a moment ago was not going to give up. Turning her face, Jericho made it where they were looking into each other's eyes. Never had she felt anything more intimate or seductive, and the power of such an action was more than she could bear. She screamed out once more. Her body felt as if it had burst apart, and in that same moment Jericho threw his head back and shuddered above her. She felt his release wash over her just as powerfully as she experienced her own, and it brought tears to her eyes.

They lay there, locked together for several heartbeats, nothing more than a heaping mass of writhing flesh. His forehead rested against hers, and they were both panting like they had run a marathon. Maybe in a way they had. Pulling away, he shifted to his side and pulled her into his arms. The cave was not the most comfortable place to sleep, but it was fine for now. At that moment, she had no complaints about anything.

"Why didn't you tell me no? Why didn't you stop me? You deserved better for your first time," he asked, his voice sounding almost defeated. Something so wonderful should not end with such hurt-filled words.

"I didn't want to stop you. I don't know. It just felt right. I feel drawn to you. Surely you can understand that. All my life, I have been alone. I don't think I would want to go another day knowing I could be close to you and turning you away," she answered, leaning over to kiss his chest where she could feel his pounding heart. His arm squeezed her, and his eyes closed, as if he was trying to fight back tears.

"I need to find my brother and his mate. I need to know they are safe and protected. If what they told me in that place is true, then he could be in a lot of danger," Jericho said, his body once again shaking. This time she was sure it was for a much different reason than their passionate embrace.

"I knew where they were not too long ago, and I'm good at tracking. We will find them. That is part of my goal. Jericho, I have heard about you for so long. You and your brother are so important to our kind. That is why I had to get you out of that place," she said, pressing in closer to him.

"That's funny. I always talk about you. You are a legend. Most don't even think you are real. Can you really shift into objects?" he asked, his eyes lighting up with childlike curiosity. Her words had given him hope, and she could feel that bringing life back into his soul.

Sitting up, she let her power wash over them, and before long, she was a thick blanket covering his naked form. She could feel when he reached out and stroked his hand over her as if trying to decide if what he had witnessed was true. If she had been able to, she would have smiled.

"This is unreal," he gasped, gathering her up and sitting up. He moved her around, folded her up in amazement, and then lay her back down so she could shift back.

"It's just me," she answered once returned to her natural form. Looking out of the opening of the cave, she realized the sun was starting to set. The wind brought the sweet scent of all the beautiful spring flowers to them. She beamed at the aroma and leaned into Jericho with a peaceful sigh. "Let's get some rest tonight. Tomorrow we will head out to find your brother. Jericho, you don't have to do this alone anymore."

She felt him smile and gather her in tightly in his embrace. She knew that this moment of peace would be short lived. Their lives were not meant to be peaceful. They were fugitives to a law that did not exist, hunted like animals. There was no rest for them, but they could take these few short moments. They both needed the rest anyway. Snuggling into his chest, her last words made her heart race. For the first time in her life, she finally felt like she was no longer alone either.

# A SLICE of Resistance Preview

"Lenora, come on. We have to move," Jax whispered in an urgent tone. Their luck had finally run out, a little later than expected.

Jax had hoped they could stay hidden until after the baby was born, but that was not going to happen. When he had gone to town, he had seen a small squad of SLICE agents questioning the locals. SLICE was short for Supernatural Laboratories for the Investigation of Chaotic Entities and very fitting for what they did. Under the guise of helping humanity, SLICE managed to hunt down and kill thousands of shifters every year. They were after genocide, and at the moment, Jax and Lenora were at the top of their priority list.

"Lenora, baby, come on. I know it's hard, but we have to get moving." Jax continued to rock his woman awake, her swollen belly shaking with every move.

This was the first time in his life Jax had been the one taking care of everything. Eight months ago, his brother had sacrificed himself to ensure Jax was able to get his woman to safety. Until that night, they had never been separated, and Jericho had always been the provider. Jax could feel his heart breaking more thinking of his brother. He had long given up the hope that Jericho was still alive. No one ever came back from a SLICE camp.

With Lenora pregnant and ready to give birth in a short amount of time, Jax knew he could no longer dream his brother would find them again. It was now time for Jax to become the man and take care of his family, which meant getting them to safety as soon as possible.

"Lenora! Now!" he barked, finally giving up on being nice. It had never been his thing before, and he did not have the time for it now.

Lenora gave a groan and pulled the blanket from over her head. On a normal day, the sight of her stretched out naked before him would send him pouncing on her, but it was not a normal day. There was no time for lovemaking.

"Why are you yelling at me? It's still early," Lenora asked as she rolled out of the bed and grabbed her robe.

"I'm yelling because you were not listening to me. We need to go. You need to get dressed," Jax answered, tossing some clothes to her as he began to pack a backpack with necessary items. They would have to travel light.

"You aren't making any sense. Why do we have to leave? I thought we were waiting for Jericho?" Lenora asked as she pulled on her clothes.

"We can't wait anymore," Jax began to explain, his gruff voice making him sound like he was growling. "SLICE agents are in town. We have to leave, now."

He saw the fear enter Lenora's eyes, and he wished he could take it away. Lenora's first experience with SLICE had been the night they had met. Since then, her whole life had been turned upside down. He knew it was his fault, too; however, he would never regret it. Had he and Jericho not taken her, she would have been captured and killed that night.

Seeing that she now understood the seriousness of the situation, Jax was able to focus on packing the things they needed most. With Lenora so close to delivering, she would not be able to carry much. He was forced to be selective in what they brought.

Filling the pack as much as he could, he then went to check on Lenora. She had on a pair of overalls and a long-sleeved green T-shirt. The overalls were the only pants she could wear that did not fall off her. Her hair had been pulled up into a ponytail, exposing her heart-shaped face and storm-colored eyes. The sight of her always stole his breath away.

"I'm sorry to have to wake you like this, but I have to keep you safe, both of you. I won't be able to live with myself if I lose any more of my family," Jax whispered, pressing his hand against her stomach as he pulled her into him for a hug. Her sweet scent tickled his nose and made him smile. Only Lenora could make him soft.

"It's okay, just don't yell at me. I'm tired. I can't help it. The baby is taking everything out of me," Lenora whispered into his neck. He could feel her rubbing her face against his scruffy beard, and a smile slid over his lips.

Jax was a large, burly man. He was broad and muscular with thick, bushy, black hair that flowed down his back and mixed with his beard. Jericho had always said he looked like an animal, which fit him well. For the most part, Jax preferred to live like an animal. When he held Lenora, however, he felt like a man. This man was in need of protecting his family. They needed to escape before the hunters found them. Giving Lenora a quick kiss, he then pulled away so he could grab the bag. Knowing everything was in order, he took her hand.

"We are going to be fine. I am not going to let anything bad happen to you. I swear it on my brother's life. He did not die in vain," Jax whispered. Jax had never admitted out loud his worries that Jericho was dead, but reality had started to set in, and he could no longer keep pretending his brother would walk through the door at any moment.

With a heavy heart and adrenaline flowing free through their blood, the two of them left the small cottage they had been living in near the beach. The small oceanside village had been a hide out for Jax and Jericho ever since their parents had died. They came every spring. Maybe that had been the problem. They had gotten careless with where they hid themselves, and SLICE had picked up on the location. It was the only thing that made any sort of sense to him.

Over the last several months, Jax had worked as a laborer, earning money for him and Lenora to live off of. With it, they had bought a car. Jax had no idea how to drive, at first, but Lenora knew and took the time to teach him. He figured it would come in handy especially now that she was further along in her pregnancy. Having Lenora use the energy to shift in her current state made Jax nervous. Though the mundane way of running was slower and forced them to take traceable paths, it was safer for his woman.

"I think we should head out of town. We can travel south and find another secluded place. It isn't safe for you to travel too much, but neither is staying here," Jax suggested as he moved into the driver's seat. The vehicle they had purchased was small and a little cramped for Jax's large form, which forced him to pull his knees up at uncomfortable angles. It certainly made driving an interesting experience for him. He wished they had been able to afford a larger car or SUV, but they had gotten what they could afford, and he was grateful for it.

"I'm not used to this, Jax. I still don't like that we have to always run. Is this how we are going to have to live all our lives? Are we going to raise our baby like this?" Lenora asked as she put her seatbelt on, and Jax headed for the main and only road out of town.

What Lenora said screamed of his own insecurity over becoming a father. Jax had no idea how to be a dad, let alone a father that could not provide a stable life for his child. Lenora had been raised in the human world. He could not just take them off to the wilderness to live like animals. She lacked the survival skills to maintain such a life. Sighing, he looked over at his beautiful woman as he drove. He had no desire to answer her question, because it would simply bring to light all of her fears, but staying silent wouldn't help the situation either.

"I know that you are not used to this, but this is how shifters are forced to live. I can't change it," Jax answered, his voice harsh.

He watched as her face hardened in anger, and then he turned back to the road. Lenora had always been a fighter. She had punched and kicked with all of her might the night they had met, and that fight had never left her. It was something he had grown to love about her. Love was not a feeling he had ever expected to experience in his life, at least not romantic love. He had plenty of love for his brother, but that was different and far less complicated than what he felt for Lenora.

The silence between them said much more than any words either of them could say. Lenora was not happy with the life she had been forced into. She had planned to live out her life in mediocrity. Now she was constantly on the run. Love or no love, it was a hard life to live, and Jax hated himself for pulling her into it.

"I would change it if I could. I would give you a better life. You know that, right?" Jax whispered the humming of the engine the only other sound in the car. The poor radio had been busted long before they had bought it, and there hadn't been money enough to have it replaced.

Lenora licked her lips, and her hands clenched in her lap. "Jax, I love you, and I will always be with you. It does not make this life any easier though. I know you would give me a better life. I know that you never planned to have the life I have given you either. We both have to make changes. I'm sorry I get so upset, but I'm afraid, and I don't like being afraid."

Reaching over, she wrapped her tiny hand around his much larger one. Her thumb stroked over his skin and soothed his worries and fears. How she did that, he would never understand. She had always calmed him in a way no one, not even his brother, had ever been able to before. It was as if she understood him more so than he even did himself. "You have every right to be upset. I dragged you into this life."

"No, you didn't drag me into this life. I was born into it. I was just lucky enough to be able to hide from it a lot longer than you. My mother did everything she could to keep me from them. To keep me safe, but there is only so long you can hide," Lenora answered, her voice soft but full of strength.

Hiding was how they had been living the last eight months. For that short period of time, Jax had gotten to remember what it was like to simply live his life and not wonder where his next meal was coming from or if he would live to see the sun rise. For far too long he had been forced to be a survivor. Now they were diving headfirst back into survival mode. There would be no more hiding for them.

The small town gave way to the highway. It would not be long before they were on the interstate headed for a new hideout. Jax was well aware the two of them could not stay on the highway long. Lenora would need to be some place safe before she went into labor. Glancing over at her, he wanted to smile, but knew it would do little good. So instead, he returned his eyes to the road and tried to relax. The silence was needed and made him able to think of what his next step would be.

# About the

# Author

Cherron Riser was born in Dothan, Alabama on November 2, 1983. With her family being military, she spent a lot of her early childhood traveling all over the country, giving her a lot of new and different experiences she would not otherwise have been given. When she turned ten, however, her family settled in the small town of Ozark, Alabama where she finished her high school career.

After high school, Cherron began college, however she also found herself in love with her old high school crush. The two of them were married in July of 2002, and welcomed their first child in October of 2003, after moving to Knoxville, Tennessee. In December 2008 the welcomed their second child and found themselves headed back to Alabama. They have now been married for over thirteen years, and Cherron has returned to school to finish what she had started all those years ago.

All through her life Cherron has been drawn to the arts. As a child she danced and sang all of the time, often driving her family crazy. During middle school, a group of friends and Cherron started "The Outcast" a club established for building a love of writing. Once the club was formed, Cherron was never seen without a spiral notebook and pen. She wrote daily, developing silly stories for her friends. After high school, Cherron began to write more serious stories and develop more original plot lines. It is a talent and love Cherron has developed over the years, filling her computer with story after story.

As an author, Cherron began her career as a self published author, releasing the book Defying Destiny in March of 2015. She gives a lot of credit to her husband, children, and friends for inspiring her characters and worlds and looks forward to showing them to all of her readers in the near future. Cherron can often be seen at conventions, both for readers and for geeks, as she is and will always be a geek herself, and proud of it.

Made in the USA
Middletown, DE
09 May 2022

65558767R00227